COMING HOME TO CRUMBLETON

CRUMBLETON BOOK 1

BETH RAIN

PROLOGUE

CRUMBLETON TIMES AND ECHO - 12TH APRIL

What's On This Week

Darts at the Dolphin & Anchor, Wednesday 7.30pm

Crumbleton darts team is on the lookout for new members! Brian says being the only member is getting boring. If darts is your thing - or if you just fancy taking out your frustrations over a pint - contact Brian Singer.

Final call for entries into the Odd Object Competition

The museum might still be closed while we continue our search for a new curator, but Crumbleton WI have stepped in to run this year's Odd Object Competition! Up to three items per entrant - bring your entries up to

CHAPTER 1

RUBY

The view from the back seat of the taxi was becoming painfully familiar. Ruby Hutchinson ran her hands up and down her thighs - doing her best to wipe the nervy clamminess from her palms while simultaneously seeking comfort from the rough grain of her jeans.

It wasn't working.

Ruby's fight or flight mechanism was well and truly stuck in "flight" mode… but that simply wasn't an option today.

Letting out a long, slow breath, Ruby leaned her forehead against the cool glass window, willing the knot of anxiety in her stomach to loosen up a bit. She knew it was just wishful thinking, though. This particular knot had been her constant companion for more than a month now. In fact, she could pinpoint the exact moment her guts had decided to twist themselves into a tangle - that fateful Wednesday morning in her editor's swanky London office.

It should have been a wonderful meeting with Harriet - after all, her editor had nothing but good news to share. About two minutes into proceedings, Ruby's entire publishing team had descended bearing balloons, champagne and a professional photographer to commemorate the moment. Her debut novel had hot-footed it right to the top of every single chart going - it was officially an international bestseller - and had already sold more than a million copies.

As the office erupted in a volley of cheers and champagne corks, Ruby had just felt hollow. She knew she should be beside herself with joy. According to everyone else, she was living the dream and her book was hitting milestones most authors could only dream of. All those long hours at her tiny desk had paid off - the late nights getting "just one more chapter" written, followed by the bleary-eyed early morning editing sessions had been worth it.

The truth was - that had been the bit she'd actually enjoyed. Writing had always given her a sanctuary from real life, and there was nothing quite like the buzz of adrenaline when the story was flowing from her fingertips. She loved it. The whole publicity side of things, however? Not so much.

Still, it was a necessary evil and she'd quickly discovered that it wasn't something she could opt out of. That was the only reason she'd agreed to embark on an international tour when all she really wanted to do was hide. It was a desire that got about a million times stronger when Harriet gleefully announced that they'd firmed up the final stop on her tour at last. They were sending Ruby back home to Crumbleton for the first time in six years – and she had absolutely no say in the matter.

Ruby closed her eyes for a moment, doing her best to block out the gleaming waterways and golden reeds of the salt marshes flying past the window. She was exhausted. A month of globe-trotting - signing thousands of books in dozens of countries and meeting scores of fans - had been overwhelming, to say the least. But none of it had made her feel as anxious as this last stop.

'Why did it have to be Crumbleton?' she whispered.

'What's that love?'

The driver's voice made Ruby jump, and she sat up quickly, feeling like an idiot.

'Nothing Brian!' she said, forcing a bright smile onto her face as she met his concerned gaze in the rear-view mirror. 'Just… nearly home. That's all!'

'We'll be there soon, right enough!' he said cheerfully, the fine lines around his eyes crinkling in a smile she couldn't quite see. 'Look - there she is - just peeping through the mist!'

Ruby leaned forward to peer through the windscreen. Yep - there she was indeed. Crumbleton was sticking up like a sore thumb out of the misty marshes.

The little town on a hill that had once been her home.

The little town she'd left behind six years ago.

The little town she'd prefer to keep avoiding for another six years… or preferably, six decades. In fact, if Ruby had her way, she'd be more than happy never to set foot on its cobbled streets again.

'Home's looking lovely this morning,' said Brian happily. 'Looks like we're in for a beautiful day too.'

Ruby nodded and slumped back in her seat. If only the sight of Crumbleton made her half as happy as Brian! She knew she should be excited - after all, she was going to get to see her parents on their home turf for the first time in forever.

'You know,' said Brian, cutting into her thoughts, 'everyone's been talking about who you've based all your characters on. Half the town reckons they're in there somewhere!'

'Well… good for them,' she sighed. The worthies of Crumbleton could wonder all they wanted, but they'd never know the truth.

'You alright back there, Rubes?'

Brian cast a concerned glance over his shoulder, and Ruby promptly forced a smile back onto her face. This was exactly the kind of thing she'd been dreading - and precisely the reason she had zero chance of flying under the radar during this visit – even the taxi driver had known her since birth.

'I'm fine, thanks,' she said, forcing herself to sound as cheerful as possible. 'I just... hate this song,' she said, quickly inventing an excuse. There was no way she was going to tell him the truth - she'd be a pariah if she said anything in the least bit negative about Crumbleton to anyone who actually lived there. 'Any chance you can turn the radio off?'

'Sure!' he said with an easy shrug, hitting the dial with a flourish. 'Anything for our home-grown celeb. I couldn't believe it when I got the booking through from your fancy-pants publisher, you know!'

Ruby felt the smile solidify on her face. 'How's Michelle?' she said quickly, desperate to steer the conversation away from anything to do with her book, her publisher, and her so-called celebrity status. She'd gone to primary school with Brian's daughter – and they'd been in the same class all the way until the end of secondary school.

'Oh, she's right happy!' said Brian, breaking into a wide smile. 'That young man of hers is something special, and they've got a lovely place. I wish they'd settled a bit closer of course, but...'

Ruby smiled and nodded along as Brian filled her in on everything from the new carpets his daughter had just fitted, to the fact she'd won a karaoke competition on the cruise she'd enjoyed the previous summer. Her plan had worked a treat. Brian's daughter had always been the apple of his eye. Combined with the fact that he could chat for Britain, Ruby was seriously hoping that his fatherly monologue might get them all the way to Crumbleton.

'You know… I should thank you,' said Brian, glancing at her again.

'Oh?' said Ruby.

'Michelle's coming back to visit this week… and it's all down to you,' said Brian.

'Me?' said Ruby, with a sinking sensation. She had a feeling they were about to stray straight back onto the topic she was most keen to avoid.

'Absolutely,' said Brian, nodding vigorously. 'She said there was no way on earth she was going to miss your event.'

'Oh,' said Ruby.

'She loved your book,' said Brian. 'I've not started it yet - but I got my copy from Crumbleton Bookshop the minute it came out. Gotta support our own!'

'Right, right…' said Ruby. 'Well… it'll be lovely to see Michelle. At least I know someone's going to be there on the day!'

'I'll be there too. I've taken the time off work specially,' said Brian. 'Can't wait. Not often we get a local celeb… and even less often they played in my back garden when they were little!'

Ruby nodded but couldn't bring herself to say anything.

'You sure you're okay, Rubes?' said Brian again after

watching her in the rear-view mirror for a long moment. 'You don't quite seem like yourself.'

Ruby raised her eyebrows. How Brian Singer knew when she was being "herself" was beyond her, considering he'd not seen her since she'd scarpered. That was the thing with Crumbleton, though. Everyone thought they knew you inside and out - and they thought they knew all your business too.

Well… that just went to show, didn't it. She was pretty confident that no one in the little town had the first clue why she'd done a disappearing act practically overnight. Other than Caroline, of course – but Caroline was her best friend and basically knew everything about everyone. That was her thing. She also happened to be *his* cousin…

'Ruby?' said Brian. 'Love… do you want me to pull over? You've gone all pale.'

Ruby shook her head quickly and gave herself a mental slap. If she wasn't careful, it'd be all over town that she was ill… or losing her marbles… or maybe both. It definitely wasn't the look she was going for!

'I'm fine, thanks Brian,' she said yet again. 'Really. I'm just a bit wiped out. It's been a busy month… I've been here, there and everywhere.'

'Must have been exciting!' he said.

'Exhausting, if I'm honest,' said Ruby with a little laugh.

'Well… you're nearly home now,' said Brian.

Ruby swallowed. His low, kind voice was making her tired eyes prickle.

'A couple of weeks at home will put everything right,' he added. 'You just need a bit of a rest somewhere you feel comfortable.'

Ruby nodded. He was right about that last bit, but how was Brian to know that Crumbleton was the last place on Earth she'd feel comfortable. It hadn't been *home* for a long time. The problem was… neither had anywhere else.

As for staying in town for a couple of weeks? There was no way. Her plan was to get the signing out of the way and then skedaddle on the first available train. With any luck, that would give her just enough time to catch up with her parents, see Caroline and maybe grab a coffee and cake in the café.

'You know, I'm surprised you're on your own, what with you being so important,' said Brian, shooting a cheeky glance at her over his shoulder, clearly trying to lighten the mood. 'How come you've not got a minder or someone tagging along?'

Ruby rolled her eyes. Brian didn't know how close to the truth he'd just come. 'Trust me, I wasn't so lucky at any of the other stops!' she said with a small smile. 'There was no getting away from my publicists!'

It hadn't been *that* bad. Bobbie and Ben from the marketing department had provided more than a little bit of light relief as she'd shlepped around Europe, before heading to Australia and then over to the States.

The double-act had kept her on her toes and stopped her from becoming a total hotel-room hermit. Still, she had to admit they were also the main reason she felt like she needed a month-long lie down in a darkened room to get over the experience.

'I basically had to beg them to let me come down here on my own,' she laughed, watching as the base of Crumbleton hill drew ever nearer.

'As if you need anyone holding your hand in Crumbleton!' chuckled Brian. 'You know the place like the back of your hand!'

'Mm hmm,' mumbled Ruby, noncommittally. She certainly did. That wasn't the reason she'd put her foot down, though. The last thing she'd needed on this trip was someone dictating her every move. She wanted to fly under the radar as much as was humanly possible - something that was an alien concept to the colourful pair. Bobbie and Ben would want to make sure her tour went out with a glitter-canon-style bang. Ruby was determined to let it slip by more like a whisper in a deserted school hall.

'Rubes, do you mind if I drop you off at the bottom of town next to the City Gates?' said Brian. 'Andy's working on fixing the cobbles up by the museum and it's impossible to turn around without about forty-seven tries… and I've got another pick-up over at Crumbleton Sands in quarter of an hour.'

'Of course!' said Ruby, nodding her head enthusiastically. Sure, it meant she'd either have to face the ankle-breaking cobbles or the many sets of steep stone steps that took you from the bottom of Crumbleton to the top - but it would definitely make it a lot easier to sneak in unannounced. Cars weren't really encouraged on the high street anyway. For one thing, it was insanely steep and narrow, and for another, any passengers tended to need a visit to the chiropractor after the bumpy trip!

'You sure? Got your sensible shoes on?' said Brian, a hint of concern in his voice.

'Always!' laughed Ruby. Flats were the default for anyone born and bred in Crumbleton. Anything else meant you were dancing with disaster! 'I've only got one bag and besides, I could do with the exercise.'

'Right you are, then,' said Brian cheerfully. 'Here we go.'

'Fab, thanks Brian,' she said, taking a deep breath and peering through the window, just to check that the coast was clear. 'How much do I owe you?'

'All sorted out with your publisher,' said Brian, beaming at her. 'Now - you enjoy being home.'

'Uh huh,' sighed Ruby, still staring out of the window.

'Ruby?' he said. 'You need a hand?'

'Sorry Brian,' she said. 'I'm going, I promise.'

'Good-oh. I thought you might be waiting for me to open the door for you. Thought maybe you'd got a bit too used to being a celebrity already!' He turned and winked at her.

Ruby widened her eyes in horror, shook her head and shoved the door open.

'Rubes!' he called, winding his window down.

'Yeah?'

'I was just joking!' he said with a kind smile.

'I know,' said Ruby.

'Hey Rubes?' he said again, looking hopeful. 'I don't suppose you play darts?'

Ruby grinned and shook her head at the familiar plea she'd heard so many times as a teen. 'Nope – sorry!'

'Ah well,' he sighed, looking disappointed. 'Had to ask.' Brian gave a little shrug, wound his window back up and with one last wave, set off to collect his next customers.

Ruby let out a long, slow breath.

Well… here she was. Back in Crumbleton.

She couldn't wait to leave.

CHAPTER 2

RUBY

Ruby stared after Brian's cab as it trundled away, heading back across the marshland in the direction of Crumbleton Sands. The urge to chase after him, waving her arms and begging to be taken straight back to the train station, was almost overwhelming.

'No such luck,' she sighed as he disappeared around a bend.

This was it then – the moment she'd been dreading for weeks. She was well and truly back in Crumbleton!

Dragging her feet, Ruby turned reluctantly to stare at the City Gates.

'City gates!' she muttered, rolling her eyes.

Crumbleton wasn't a city by any stretch of the imagination. It was a small town crammed onto a steep hill that stuck out of the surrounding salt marshes. Once upon a time, it had been a lot closer to the sea, but over the centuries the marshes had grown, the waves had receded, and Crumbleton had been left high and dry with nothing but its nautical-sounding house names to remind it of its coastal history.

Ruby stared at the huge stone archway with its wooden gates covered in a jumble of signs warning motorists that the high street was "access only". Without thinking about it, she reached out and patted the rough stonework, before snatching her hand back in confusion as a strange rush of sensation threw her off kilter. She sucked in a sharp breath. Her hand tingled with a sense of deep recognition, almost as though the ancient, sun-warmed stone was welcoming her home.

'Don't lose the plot now, Rubes,' she muttered, giving herself a little shake for acting like a goggle-eyed tourist. Plenty of visitors stopped next to the gates every single day during the summer season - keen to get a selfie in front of the well-known site. Locals barely even noticed it was there, though – to them, it was just part of the landscape. She'd clearly been away for too long.

'Or not long enough,' she whispered, glancing at it one more time before scuttling through into Crumbleton.

Ruby's plan was to head straight to her parents' place where she could dump her bag and go to ground for a couple of hours. But first... she had to choose which route to take. She could follow the main road -

the winding, cobbled high street that led from Downhill to Uphill. It was probably the fastest route, but it also meant she'd have to walk past every single business in town. It had to be the quickest way to announce her return that Ruby could think of.

'Steps it is, then!' she murmured, setting off in the direction of the vast, white frontage of the Dolphin and Anchor hotel, before turning up a narrow pathway that led between two ancient, crooked cottages.

Crumbleton was full of little passages like this - secret cut-throughs that invariably consisted of some of the steepest steps she'd ever come across. They tended to be uneven, and narrow and usually boasted clumps of wildflowers and grasses growing between the old stones. Still - they made navigating your way around Crumbleton a whole lot easier when the place was swarming with tourists… or when you were trying to avoid someone or…

Or when you're sneaking off to meet a boy no one knows about!

Ruby shook her head to dislodge that particular memory before it had the chance to take root like the clump of dandelions she'd just stepped over. She'd promised herself she wouldn't waste any time thinking about *him!* It had happened years ago, and she was over it.

Over it.

She was over it.

Kind of.

The fact that she hadn't been back to Crumbleton for so long had nothing to do with him. Nothing at all. She was a big girl now - an internationally known author. There was no way she was still broken-hearted over a boy she'd known at school.

'He wishes,' she huffed, noting that her heart was hammering - which had everything to do with the steep steps she was now climbing and absolutely nothing to do with the memories of toned arms, a cheeky smile and stolen kisses that were doing their best to break through her defences.

Ruby sped up, determined to punish herself for letting him into her head so soon after arriving back in town. It was ridiculous. After all - he didn't even live there anymore. Hell, he'd left Crumbleton before her. There was no reason on Earth she'd bump into him now.

Ruby shook her head in annoyance and grabbed hold of the age-worn metal railing to haul herself up a particularly steep section of steps. This was *exactly* why she'd avoided Crumbleton all these years. Every single nook and cranny held memories. Most of them good. A few of them sweet. But some of them… some of them were so painful it felt like she was being run-through with a sword.

'Idiot,' she puffed, pausing as she came to a little cobbled yard – a break between one set of steps and the next. In true Crumbleton style, it was crammed with planters bursting with colourful flowers. Just because it wasn't on the main route through the town didn't mean that it didn't deserve love, attention and a dash of colour. Orange marigolds and deep blue cornflowers bobbed in the light breeze, welcoming her to their little hidey-hole. After a couple of seconds, Ruby had her breathing back under control.

Good. Okay, she could do this.

One more steep flight, then she could take the narrow passageway between Phyllis Taylor's cottage and the bridal shop and she'd almost be at her parents' house.

Just the thought of seeing them again brought a smile back to her face – though it hadn't been that long since their last visit. Ruby's mum and dad made a point of travelling to London fairly often – but she never got to see much of them while they were there. They always arrived with an itinerary that was so jam-packed with museum visits, concerts and exhibitions that Ruby was forced to tag along just to get some time with them. Her parents had always been like that, though - completely caught up in their own interests. Sure, they loved her - and she knew that – but it had always been in their own, slightly distracted way.

It was one of the things that had made it so easy for her to read and write the majority of her teenage years away. Except for that last summer, of course. That's when she'd quickly discovered her parents' preoccupation with their own interests made it super-easy to sneak away to meet boys… or, in her case, one boy in particular!

'Nope, nope, nope!' chanted Ruby as she took the next few steps at a jog. If only running away from her memories was quite so easy!

There wasn't a handrail along this stretch, and the steps were flanked on either side by thick greenery. Trimmed shrubs created leafy walls - and she paused as something shiny caught her eye. Reaching out, Ruby plucked the strange item out of the hedge and snorted. Nothing changed! It was an ornate brass doorknob. Another couple of steps up, she found a bit of metal scrolling that looked like it had fallen off an antique bureau, and on the next step sat an ancient key.

Ruby bent down to retrieve it and turned it over in her fingers with a grin. She'd had a collection of bits and pieces like this on her bedroom windowsill as a kid – gathered over the years she'd climbed these steps almost every day. They'd always been a treasure trove of weird and wonderful finds… and for good reason.

Right at the very top of Crumbleton, on the crest of the hill, was the castle and a museum… and next door was an antique shop. Geraldine, the loud, chatty owner, knew exactly what she was doing when it came to re-stocking and deliveries. She navigated the steep hill in her van after midnight - like some kind of antiquarian night owl. After restocking the shop with finds from the local salerooms, she'd pile the van high with that week's deliveries and then hotfoot it back out of town while everyone was still in bed.

The problem was every time she sold something to one of the tourists who'd travelled from further afield – they tended to want to take their purchases away with them there and then. This caused a logistical nightmare - especially if it was one of the larger pieces of furniture. Technically, you were allowed to drive up the hill for pick-ups and deliveries – but the narrow street only had one or two passing places. On a busy day, not even the most determined person could manage it - there simply wasn't enough room. This left one option – the item had to be carried all the way down to the bottom.

Of course, no one in their right mind wanted to play dodgems with all the people wandering around, enjoying the sights while carrying a heavy piece of furniture over the uneven cobbles – so the various cut-throughs and steps saw more than their fair share of antiques. Being so narrow and difficult to navigate, they tended to end up with a liberal scattering of keys, knobs, hinges and brackets in the process.

In fact…

'Uh oh!' chuckled Ruby, pocketing the key as she spotted someone walking backwards down the steps towards her. Judging by his awkward gait and weird angle, it looked like he was carrying something seriously heavy.

Ruby knew she should get out of the way as quickly

as possible before she got mown down - but something about the sight of the perfect, denim-clad behind reversing towards her seemed to have hit the pause button in her brain.

A second guy appeared around the bend, struggling with his own end of the heavy steamer trunk they were carrying between them. His eyes grew wide the minute he spotted her, clearly realising that a pile-up was imminent.

'Wow!' he shouted, yanking them both to an abrupt halt.

The sharp, warning cry made Ruby come out of her ogle-trance.

'Sorry!' she muttered, shaking her head. 'I'll back up!'

'Either that or you could try crawling under?' puffed the man, sounding exhausted but not unfriendly.

Ruby raised her eyebrows, but she only considered the suggestion for the briefest moment. The guy's face was pink with exertion and he was sweating. As for Mr Prefect-Bum, he hadn't even turned his head to glance in her direction. He was clearly having to use every ounce of his remaining energy to keep a grip on the giant trunk – and his arms were shaking.

'I'll get out of your way!' she said. Turning quickly, she trotted back down the uneven steps as fast as her legs would carry her. She didn't stop until she reached the bright little cobbled yard where she could take a step back towards the planters and squeeze out of their path when they finally caught up with her.

'Cheers!'

Ruby started to shrug, but she froze mid-gesture.

That voice!

It had come from Mr Cute-Bottom. Ruby shivered as a blast from the past sent chills down her spine. She quickly looked down at her feet. She wasn't sure if it was because she'd be horrified if it really *was* him… or disappointed if it wasn't.

Ruby's ears started to whistle, and she stared hard at the cobbles, waiting for them to squeeze past so that she could leg it up the rest of the steps and away from them as quickly as possible.

'Love, are you okay?'

The concerned voice made her peep up at the second guy, who'd paused right in front of her.

'Grand thanks!' she said, forcing herself to look at him and not the other guy who was mere feet away from her. He was close enough that she could hear him breathing.

'Okay… if you're sure,' he said. 'You just look a bit… white? Like you've seen a ghost.'

'Thanks… I'm fine,' she said again with a tight smile. 'Long journey, that's all. Looking forward to a cuppa.'

'Straight to Crumbleton Café with you, then,' he said. 'There's a cut-through to the high street a bit further up the steps.'

Ruby smiled and nodded. She knew exactly where

Crumbleton Café was - of course she did, considering she'd worked there for years.

'Can we get on with it, my fingers are going to drop off!'

The grumble made every hair on Ruby's body stand on end as memories started to swirl around her, like she was trapped inside a snow globe of her past.

'Fine,' the man gave her a wink. 'Let's go!'

Ruby gave him an awkward smile as he shuffled past, and then mustering every ounce of her willpower, she took off up the steps like a whippet. How she managed to stop herself from glancing back over her shoulder to see if her gut instinct was correct was anyone's guess.

Panting as she sprinted up the last few steps, Ruby shook her head. She'd spent years trying to avoid this… *him*… surely there was no way all that effort had come to nothing just minutes after arriving back in town?

But… that voice…

No – she had to be wrong! She'd probably just imagined him into being because she'd been dreading coming back here and facing the memories.

But what if it *was* him?

Oliver Evans couldn't be back in Crumbleton… could he?!

CHAPTER 3

OLI

Oli sucked in a long, slow breath, trying to will his hands to stop shaking. It had nothing to do with the weight of the heavy trunk he was carrying and everything to do with the human roadblock they'd just had to edge past on the narrow stairway.

He'd known exactly who it was the second he heard her voice. Ruby Hutchinson was back in Crumbleton. Of course - it wasn't exactly a surprise that she was back in town. What *was* a huge surprise was his reaction to her. He'd kept his eyes down the entire time... but not looking at Ruby hadn't helped. His entire body had just reacted to being so close to her again after so many years.

It was no good. Oli's arms were shaking, his heart pounding, and his breath was coming in short gasps.

'Can we take a sec?' he grunted, before setting his

end of the trunk down on the next available spot to shake out his hands.

'Dude - you okay?' asked Lee, following suit before staring at him with a raised eyebrow. 'Crikey - you need to get back to training if carrying this little thing is proving to be a bit much.'

Oli smirked at his friend and rolled his shoulders, playing up the ready-made excuse he'd just been handed for all he was worth. The last thing he needed was for his piss-taking mate to figure out that his current predicament had nothing to do with carrying the heavy piece of furniture down the hill, and everything to do with a certain famous author they'd just seen sneaking into town via the back route!

'I'll be fine in a sec,' huffed Oli, willing his heart to calm the actual eff down.

Of course, he'd known that he'd be bumping into Ruby in the next few days… but he'd planned the encounter down to the finest detail. He knew exactly what he wanted to say and how he wanted to say it. He'd make it light and breezy – like it didn't still bother him that he'd been so in love with her six years ago, he'd flown to America with nothing but her face in his head. Like he hadn't been replaying their final moments over and over again for far longer than was sane.

It had taken him a while, but Oli had forgiven her for cutting him out of her life so completely. After all, they'd both been kids at the time. What hope did two eighteen-year-olds have of keeping a long-distance relationship alive when they were up against adults who thought they knew better. Or - one particular adult in this case!

Still, seeing Ruby back in Crumbleton after all this time was bound to stir things up again, wasn't it?!

'Dude, was that Ruby Hutchinson?'

Lee's voice made Oli jump. He'd been so lost in the past that he'd almost forgotten where he was for a second.

'Erm... might have been?' said Oli with a small shrug, his heart renewing its ridiculous pounding at her name on Lee's lips. 'Didn't really get a proper look - I was too busy trying not to drop this stupid thing,' he added, toeing the trunk.

'You definitely need to lay off the pastries and get back in shape!' chuckled Lee. 'Crumbleton's clearly not doing your reputation as a racing snake any good!'

'I'm a reformed racing snake!' said Oli. 'I'm allowed as much cake as I can fit in these days.'

'Fair enough,' said Lee. 'The fatter you get, the cuter I look standing next to you.'

Oli snorted and rolled his eyes. Lee had always been a bit of an idiot - and not much had changed since they'd been on the school football team together. Still, it had been a nice surprise to discover that his old friend still lived in Crumbleton. He was easy company and always up for a pint at the end of the week.

'I remember Ruby from school, you know,' said Lee. 'Always thought she was pretty cute… for a total nerd.'

'Mmm,' said Oli, hoping the noncommittal grunt might signal just how uninterested he was in talking about how cute or nerdy Ruby had been at school. It was dangerous territory and Lee was like a terrier with a bone if he caught even the slightest whiff of potential gossip. Oli had managed to keep this particular secret for a very long time and he didn't much fancy letting it slip out now!

'I mean, obviously, I wouldn't have done anything about it,' said Lee, glancing up the steps with a raised eyebrow, as though he was chasing after Ruby in his mind's eye, 'but nerds are more acceptable now, right?'

'Maybe,' muttered Oli, 'but that was a long time ago. She's probably married with a bunch of kids by now.'

'Eww!' huffed Lee. 'But still… she's pretty cute…'

Oli grabbed his end of the trunk and hefted it so that Lee had no choice but to take his own end again. With any luck, it would distract him enough to make him shut up and drop the subject. Oli really didn't need a trip down memory lane where Lee decided to retrospectively lust after his ex-girlfriend… or ex-*whatever* Ruby was to him.

They'd never really put a label on what had happened between them. They'd never told anyone about it either – other than Caroline of course – but they hadn't had much choice when it came to her. She was Ruby's best friend - and *his* cousin. Add to that the fact she was also the nosiest person in Crumbleton and they hadn't stood a chance of keeping it from her. Luckily enough, Caroline was also loyal to a fault and knew how to keep a secret.

It had been a magical summer – one where the pair of them rarely left their happy little bubble-for-two. Of course, the summer had ended with his first and only broken heart. Still – his time with Ruby had changed his life forever. He couldn't deny that.

'Dude, you sure you're okay?' said Lee, a look of real concern on his face as they continued their tortuous shuffle down the hill.

'I'm fine!' huffed Oli, taking another treacherous step backwards.

'But… you're puffing again, and you're all red in the face!' said Lee.

'Just cursing Andy for choosing today of all days to work on that wonky patch of cobbles. If anything should be moved with the help of a van, it's this monstrosity!'

Of course, his discomfort had nothing whatsoever to do with the three hundred steps they still had to face until they'd be able to load the blasted thing into the van waiting for them in the Dolphin and Anchor's carpark. It *did* however have everything to do with the fact that right now, Ruby was probably heading to her parents' house. Then she'd be wandering around

Crumbleton... visiting the café... visiting the bookshop...

'I can't believe she's back!'

Oops. That particular thought had escaped his lips.

Lee raised an eyebrow at him. 'Right?' he said. 'Who'd have thought someone that successful would come back to this hole!'

'Oi,' huffed Oli. 'I happen to love this hole.'

'Of course you do,' chuckled Lee. 'But then, it turns out you're as big a nerd as she is! Like... a nerd in jock's clothing. Hey - maybe if she isn't married and doesn't have babies, you two nerds can get together and have little nerdletts!'

Oli promptly lost his grip on the trunk and almost dropped it on his toes.

'Dude - watch it!' laughed Lee. 'Seriously man - you need to start working out more.'

'You know, you don't *have* to keep asking for my help whenever your grandmother sells something heavy and ropes you in to carry it down the hill!' grunted Oli.

'You know you love me really,' said Lee with a grin.

'Yeah... somewhere very deep down,' sighed Oli, taking a deep breath before getting a better grip on the trunk. He needed to focus on what he was doing before one of them ended up getting hurt.

And there it was - the root of the problem. Whenever Ruby Hutchinson was anywhere near him,

Oli lost his head... then his heart... and then he got hurt.

Well, at least their little encounter had sorted one thing out - six years apart hadn't been quite the cure he'd been hoping for!

CHAPTER 4

RUBY

*R*uby burst onto the cobbled high street, almost mowing down a little old lady in the process.

'Steady on there, dear!' said the woman, clutching Ruby's arm - though whether it was to steady Ruby or herself was up for debate.

'I'm so sorry!' puffed Ruby, bringing her hand to her heart as though she might be able to calm both its erratic fluttering and the deep ache that seemed to have appeared out of nowhere.

'No harm done,' said the woman, peering closely at her. 'Well, well, well, if it isn't our very own Ruby!'

Ruby straightened up and took a better look at her victim's face. 'Mrs Barker!' she said, recognition dawning… and noting with relief that this time it came with a warm bloom of affection rather than horror.

'The one and only!' said the woman, her face

creasing like a paper bag as she grinned at Ruby. 'I have to say, I can't wait for your event. Got my ticket the minute they came out!'

'Oh!' said Ruby, not sure what else to say to say. 'Erm… thank you. That's nice.'

She'd had plenty of time to get used to the fact that people were reading her book. Of *course* they were… after all, it *was* a bestseller that had already sold over a million copies. Still, she'd somehow managed to convince herself that no one in Crumbleton would be interested. Ruby knew it was ridiculous – but it had been the only way she'd managed to stay vaguely sane about the whole thing.

A sudden swoop of nerves hit her square in the chest. People in Crumbleton had been reading her book!

Somehow, speaking to huge crowds all over the world had been manageable, because they were mostly faceless - a bunch of strangers she could put on an act for. There was no chance she was going to be able to pull off the same thing here though, was there? The majority of people in Crumbleton had known her all her life.

What had she let herself in for?! She should have put her foot down and never agreed to come back – especially not as part of her book tour!

'Ruby?' said Mrs Barker, frowning at her in concern. 'Are you quite alright, dear?'

Ruby nodded quickly, doing her best to act as normal as possible and swallow down her panic.

'I just took the steps a bit too fast, that's all,' she said, forcing a smile onto her face. It wasn't a total lie – though she'd keep the real reason she'd just pelted up the steps like a hyperactive gazelle to herself. 'I guess I'm just a bit out of practice!'

'Ah well, you'll get the hang of it again before you know it!' said the old woman, patting her hand. 'Now then, I'll let you go. Your mum will never forgive me if I keep you gossiping before she's had the chance to see you!'

Ruby just smiled and nodded, though she doubted her parents had even clocked that she was due back today. She had no doubt they'd be pleased to see her – they always were – but there was never any urgency or excitement around it.

A sudden wave of guilt threatened to take her out at the knees at the thought. She was *lucky* to have such wonderful parents. It wasn't a big deal that they tended to be preoccupied, was it?! She knew they loved her. Deep down.

Ruby took a deep breath as she watched Mrs Barker continue her slow trek up the hill. She was feeling more than a little bit off-balance – like she was a huge sack of emotions ready to burst at the seams. As much as she was looking forward to seeing her parents, she could really do with getting her head screwed back on first. They might be dithery, but they weren't stupid –

they'd know something was up – and then she'd be in for the Spanish Inquisition!

'Hi Ruby!' came a cheerful voice from across the narrow, cobbled street. 'Long time, no see!'

She raised her hand to wave, half in a daze, only to spot her old primary school caretaker smiling at her.

'Loved your book!' came a female voice from her side of the street.

'Oh - hi!' said Ruby, blinking at Grace, the mother of an old school friend. 'Erm… thanks!'

'I'll be there to get it signed!' she said with a bright smile. 'Good to have you home!'

Ruby smiled and nodded on autopilot, feeling her eyes grow wide. This was going to get overwhelming… and fast. She needed to get off the high street and gather her wits about her before she was tempted to do another - very public - runner.

'Gotta nip up to the bookshop to say hi!' she said.

'Of course,' said Grace, wiggling her eyebrows. 'Bet you can't wait!'

'Erm… right?' said Ruby, frowning slightly. What on earth did she mean by that?! 'See you…?'

Grace nodded, giving her a friendly wave as she headed off down the hill.

Well, at least her spur-of-the-moment excuse had made Ruby's mind up as to her first stop. She was going to have to visit the bookshop now, whether she wanted to or not. Still, it wouldn't be a bad idea to nip in and let Reuben know she'd arrived in town.

Hoisting her bag more securely onto her shoulder, Ruby turned her steps uphill, nodding and smiling at various people as she went. The sun always brought people to Crumbleton - and today was no exception. Several of the shops had their doors propped open to make the most of the early summer sunshine.

This was Crumbleton at its very best... and an overwhelming wave of love for the old place took Ruby by surprise. Even after six years away, it was all just so familiar - from the crooked buildings clinging higgledy-piggledy to the hill, to the ankle-breaking but picturesque cobbles beneath her feet. Every single inch of this town was steeped in memories... and not all of them were bad, no matter what she'd been telling herself all these years.

Ruby wandered past the bridal shop, stealing a glance at the window display as she went. She'd wager her next royalty cheque that the mannequin was still wearing the same dress as the last time she'd strolled through town. The pastel interior beyond looked sweet and inviting, and a row of tiaras on a white, antique armoire glittered in the sunshine as she strolled on by.

Next came the bakery, and the scent of warm cinnamon and allspice teased her nose. Ruby's stomach instantly started to growl, and a grin crept onto her face. She'd always joked with her parents that the bakery pumped the scent onto the high street day and night - just to ensure a steady stream of customers. It was practically impossible to resist! Perhaps she'd nip in before she headed home and grab them all a bun... but right now, she was going to see Reuben.

Ruby had her fingers crossed that setting foot inside the old bookshop might help her feel less anxious about her impending signing. After all, Crumbleton Bookshop was more than familiar to her. Hell, she'd spent every moment she could in there as a kid... and every penny of her pocket money had been used to fatten up Reuben's till!

The glossy, dark green paintwork with its gorgeous gold lettering appeared ahead of her, and she felt like she was looking at a long-lost friend. The double-fronted shop had an old-school charm about it, much like Reuben himself - and she was glad to see that it hadn't changed a jot while she'd been away.

Ruby paused to admire the first window. Reuben had gone to town with a romance display to rival that of any of the big London stores. Hell - this wouldn't look out of place on the most curated of social media profiles. Dozens of bright books with their illustrated covers were framed by a stunning array of fresh flowers. Ruby smiled – this was classic Crumbleton at work. The business community was tight-knit, and the little florist at the top of town had clearly teamed up with Reuben to work some magic in the bookshop.

Mooching over to take a look at the second window display, Ruby pulled a face. This one was just as skilfully dressed, but she couldn't say she liked the fact that the centrepiece was an awful, life-sized cut-out of herself.

'Urgh, *why?!*' she murmured, only just reining in the temptation to stick her tongue out at it. These blasted things had been haunting her every move during the tour. There had even been one in the window of the small-town bookshop she'd visited in Australia.

The idea of facing a full-sized photograph of herself had never sat well with Ruby, but it was made about a million times worse by the fact that she couldn't stand the photograph. The shoot had been set up by her marketing team, and she'd hated every second of it. Bobbi and Ben had insisted on a full, heavy face of make-up and that - combined with the bright blond highlights they'd talked her into – meant that it didn't really look anything like her. Especially as she'd had a hairdresser in Paris return her hair to something resembling its natural colour since then!

Ruby sighed and turned away from the awful thing to give the door a tug. It didn't budge.

'Back in five minutes!' she muttered, noticing a little card stuck to the glass with blu-tac. 'Great!'

Well… in that case, she'd just have to go to the café. She really wasn't ready to face her mum and dad yet, and she could really do with a hit of Mabel's industrial-strength coffee right now.

Heading back down the hill again, Ruby hurried past the bakery and the bridal shop, and then all but jogged towards the door of the gorgeous, cream-fronted café. Its curved, glass windows twinkled at her, and the sound of the tinkling bell announcing her arrival made Ruby feel like she was hurtling back in time.

The moment she stepped inside, the scent of coffee and bacon sandwiches assaulted her senses. Ruby felt her shoulders relax. Now this was a dose of familiarity she could deal with.

There wasn't anyone behind the counter, but the place was pretty busy. Ruby's eyes darted around the little tables out of pure habit - checking to see if anyone was waiting to be served. She might not have worked in Crumbleton Café for years - but tell that to her instincts!

'If it isn't my best-ever waitress!'

Ruby swung around only to find Mabel Leonard scurrying towards her from the kitchen.

'Mabel!' she cried, a genuine smile splitting her face as her old boss stopped right in front of her, beaming.

'Good to see you, Ruby. It's been too long!'

Ruby nodded. She might not have wanted to come back to Crumbleton - but when it came to the café and Mabel… she was inclined to agree. It *had* been too long.

'It's lovely to see you,' said Ruby, grabbing Mabel's hand and giving it a squeeze as she glanced around again. 'The place looks great… but… are you on your own?'

Mabel rolled her eyes and nodded. 'The new girl

didn't turn up,' she sighed. 'They don't make staff like they used to,' she added, shooting a wink at Ruby.

Ruby grinned. She'd always been a favourite with Mabel. In fact, when her edits got particularly tough, she'd fantasised about being back in Crumbleton Café - working for pocket money, coffee and leftover cake.

'I'm a bit behind with this lot,' muttered Mabel, nodding at the busy café, 'but I'm sure you remember how to use the machine if you want to help yourself to a coffee.'

'Sure you don't mind?' said Ruby.

'Sure?' laughed Mabel, 'you'd be doing me a favour, girl. I'll be right with you as soon as I've finished off the order for table four.'

'Okay,' laughed Ruby, following her behind the counter.

'Oh, and while you're at it, could you take some cutlery over to them for me?' called Mabel before disappearing back through to the kitchen.

CHAPTER 5

RUBY

Chuckling to herself, Ruby stashed her rucksack into the cubby hole beneath the counter. Then, she shook her hair back and tied it up into a quick ponytail before pulling on an apron and washing her hands.

'Time warp!' she whispered to herself, as the years fell away and she was suddenly a teenager again, turning up for her weekend shift with nothing to worry about other than A-levels, essays and boys.

Grabbing two sets of cutlery and a condiment rack, Ruby made her way over to table four - vaguely dreading being recognised by one of the customers. There was no fear of that when she reached the table, though. The faces that glanced briefly up at her were strangers, and they barely even took her in before continuing what was clearly a mother-daughter argument about what colour bridesmaid's dresses would best compliment the mother of the bride's outfit. It sounded like mum was definitely winning.

Ruby quickly set everything on the table and then scuttled back to the counter. She was desperate for that coffee!

'Hello old girl,' she murmured to the ancient machine as she loaded up a puck with grounds. 'Remember me?'

As soon as the aromatic, dark brown stream had finished trickling from the silver spouts, Ruby set to frothing her jug of milk. Her mouth was now watering for the first, much-needed sip.

Visiting the café had been the perfect way to calm down and get her feet back underneath her. She'd belonged behind this counter for so many years, and now - for the first time since the book tour had kicked off - she actually felt like herself.

Quickly cleaning the milk spout, Ruby tapped the jug neatly on the countertop before pouring herself the perfect latte. She even managed to execute her signature dove in the froth.

'Not lost your touch after all!' she murmured, admiring her handiwork.

The tinkling bell above the door made her turn with a warm smile, ready to greet the newcomer. The smile promptly froze on her lips. Red-faced and slightly sweaty, her past was staring at her from the doorway.

Ruby blinked.

So... she hadn't been mistaken. Oliver Evans *was* in Crumbleton... and he was walking straight towards her.

'You're new!' he said, raising an eyebrow.

Ruby blinked again, her mouth dropping open - but no sound came out.

'I could do with a coffee?' he said. 'Like... I'm desperate!'

Ruby gaped at him, feeling like a stranded goldfish. Did he really not recognise her?

'I can talk you through the machine if you're still learning?' he said, giving her a small smile.

'I... I...' stuttered Ruby.

How was this even happening? She'd wasted hours and hours of her life obsessing about what she'd say if she ever bumped into Oli again. Now here he was - standing right in front of her - and he didn't even recognise her?!

'I...?' she stuttered again.

'Oh... never mind!' he said, glancing down at her freshly made latte. 'I'll just grab this one. I'm sure Mabel won't mind.'

Ruby watched in frozen horror as Oli picked up *her* coffee, took a sip and then cocked his head.

'You know, that's not bad - for an early attempt,' he said, shooting her a wink. Then he turned on his heel with the cup clutched in his hand and disappeared back outside, leaving the saucer on the counter.

'It's - it's not a takeaway!' she squeaked as the door banged closed behind him.

Ruby shook her head. Had that really just happened? She'd spoken to Oli for the first time in six years - and he hadn't even recognised her?! She couldn't work out if she was angry or if she just needed a damn good cry.

Blinking hard, Ruby turned away from the door. She quickly emptied and then refilled the coffee puck, before shoving it back into the machine. Then she stepped back and just stared blindly at it.

How could he have forgotten her?

'Forgotten how to use the machine?!' chuckled Mabel, as she reappeared from the kitchen.

Ruby turned to her but didn't say anything.

'Blimey my girl, you look like you've seen a ghost!' said Mabel, frowning in concern.

A stiff smile forced its way onto Ruby's face. That was the second time she'd heard those in the last hour… and she had a feeling it wasn't going to be the last.

'Here, take this over to table four for me,' she said, plonking a tray bearing a plate of toasted tea cakes drowning in melted butter onto the counter. 'I'll make that drink for you. I don't trust you around hot steam – not when you look like you're about to fall over!'

'Thanks Mabel!' muttered Ruby, picking up the tray. 'Erm… could you make it a takeaway? I need to head up to the bookshop.'

'Of course, love!' said Mabel. 'Can't expect a celebrity to wait on tables all afternoon, can I?'

'Trust me, I think I'd prefer to stay here and help you,' said Ruby as she edged around the counter.

Ruby quickly delivered the tasty treat to the mother and daughter at table four, who were still so busy debating the merits of peach over lilac that they didn't spare her a second glance.

'Here,' said Mable, placing the large paper cup down on the counter as Ruby returned and started to reluctantly shrug out of her apron.

'Sure you'll be alright on your own?' she said.

'Trust me, girl,' laughed Mabel, 'it's not the first time I've manned this place on my lonesome, and I'm sure it won't be the last. But - you're always welcome. I've missed you - you always were my favourite!'

Ruby gave Mabel a smile that was worryingly wobbly and felt around in her pockets for her wallet.

'Don't you dare!' scolded Mabel.

'You sure?' said Ruby, hesitating, even though she knew full well that when Mabel said "no", she meant it!

'Shoo!' said Mabel. 'I'll see you at your signing if not before.'

∼

The minute Ruby stepped out of the café, she paused and peered cautiously up and down the street. Now she knew for sure that Oli was in town, she was going to have to keep her wits about her. He might not have recognised her, but the last thing she needed was to keep bumping into him left, right and centre.

Maybe - if she was really lucky - he was just back for the day... but then, if that was the case surely he wouldn't have just wandered off with one of Mabel's china coffee cups!

Ruby shrugged and did her best to pull herself together. She was sure she'd be able to winkle the information out of Reuben – or even her parents if push came to shove. They'd both adored Oli – though they'd only ever known him as the lad who'd needed their daughter's help with his English Literature assignments. As far as they were concerned, she'd been his tutor and nothing more... and if she was honest, that was the way she'd like to keep it.

At least there was no sign of him on the high street. Right now, she figured her best bet was to stick to her plan. Ruby retraced her steps back towards the bookshop, crossing her fingers that Reuben would have returned from his little break.

The minute she reached the door, she let out a sigh of relief. The card had disappeared, and the old wooden sign had been flipped back to "open".

Letting herself in, Ruby found herself bathed in the golden light of one of her favourite places on earth. She'd found her love of words between these floor-to-ceiling shelves. Reuben had always favoured an old-fashioned look for his beautiful shop - complete with rolling, wooden ladders. Ruby had spent many a happy moment pretending to be Belle in the Beast's library... not that Reuben was a beast. He was a lovely old grandfather figure with a penchant for waistcoats and cord trousers.

Right now, though, her favourite bookish pseudo-grandparent was nowhere to be seen. In fact, there didn't seem to be a soul in the place. Ruby shrugged. Spending a few extra minutes perusing the books definitely wasn't any kind of hardship!

Shifting her heavy bag off of her shoulder, Ruby placed it down on the floor next to a familiar patchwork armchair. It still sat in its little alcove near the window boasting the hideous cut-out of her own face. She wrinkled her nose at it for a moment, and then decided the best thing to do was pretend it didn't exist. Sometimes denial was the only way to go!

Making her way past a large, circular table that was piled high with glossy copies of her own book, Ruby headed towards the small section of antique books at the back of the shop. She'd always loved them - especially the ornate, cloth-bound editions. Of course, she'd never had the cash as a teenager to be able to afford these collectables, but she'd always loved to look. One of her most precious possessions was the gorgeous 1894 peacock edition of Pride and Prejudice Reuben had given her for her eighteenth birthday.

Running a finger along the spines of a whole shelf full of classic cream and orange paperbacks, Ruby stopped in front of the little glass cabinet where Reuben housed his most valuable finds.

'Ooh, you beauty!' she breathed, her breath fogging the glass as she peered at a stunning, gold-embossed edition of Persuasion. She really was a sucker for anything Austen, but Persuasion had always held a special place in her heart. After all, it was one of the set books she'd helped Oli study.

Ruby eyeballed the copy for several long seconds... she had a feeling she might be heading back to London with a heavier bag – and a lighter wallet! Her fingers itched to open the case for a better look – but she knew from long experience that it would be locked. She'd just have to wait for Reuben to appear and produce the key... unless he still kept it in the ornate ashtray on his desk, of course!

Grinning with excitement, Ruby dashed back through the shop. She knew for a fact that Reuben wouldn't mind if she helped herself to a proper look inside the case. Coming to a halt in front of the desk, she instantly spotted the ashtray – exactly where it had always been.

'Bingo!' she breathed, grabbing the little key. She was about to head straight back to the case when something made her pause.

Ruby frowned. The key might have been in the right place... and the old desk was definitely the same one... but instead of Reuben's ancient ledger, there was a sleek-looking laptop. That wasn't the only change, either. Instead of the usual pile of Reuben's favourite murder-mystery paperbacks, there was a...

'No way!' she gasped.

It was an e-reader.

Ruby had nothing against them - she had two herself - one full to bursting and the other rapidly heading the same way. But the idea of Reuben owning one was... was... like a pharaoh using wifi. As for that computer instead of the stained book of numbers and fancy fountain pen...

Ruby frowned, her eyes flitting over the rest of the desk, searching for more clues as to what was going on.

'Nooo!' she gasped as they came to rest on a half-drunk cup of coffee.

Reuben drank tea, not coffee... and this particular cup was missing a saucer. What's more, it had the Crumbleton Café logo on the side.

Ruby stared at the cup as if it was a dangerous animal, ready to attack. She could just make out the remains of a wonky dove in the froth.

'Oli!' she gasped.

'That's me!' came a low voice from just behind her.

Turning slowly, Ruby came face to *still-slightly-red* face with the man who'd stalked her nightmares and her dreams for more than half a decade.

'You!' she gasped.

'Me!' said Oli, looking amused.

'What the hell are you doing here?' she spat, her confusion forcing her to go on the defensive.

'Erm… well…' Oli frowned, his face mirroring her own confusion as he ruffled his hair, making it stand up in dark, glossy spikes, 'I kind of own the place?'

CHAPTER 6

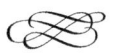

OLI

'You finished your shift in the café, then?' said Oli, quickly recovering from the shock.

She was here!

He couldn't help the grin that slid onto his face.

'How did it go? Mastered your latte art yet?'

He watched as Ruby's jaw dropped, and it was as much as he could do to stop himself from laughing out loud. She looked… indignant. Clearly, the idea that he still hadn't twigged who she was was driving her a little bit nuts.

Not that he felt *too* bad about it. After zero contact from her since the moment he'd boarded his flight to America all those years ago - Oli was surprised to find that he was more than happy to wind her up a bit.

'So… how can I help?' he said, raising his eyebrows and doing his best to look as innocent as possible.

Ruby just stared at him for a long moment, not saying anything. She looked like she was having to rein in the desire to grab him and give him a good shake. Oli picked up his cup of stolen coffee and took a long, leisurely sip, not taking his eyes off her.

'If this is a joke,' Ruby growled at last, 'it's not funny.'

Oli swallowed the mouthful of coffee and returned the cup slowly to his desk. When he looked back up at her, he couldn't stop himself from smiling.

'Sorry,' he chuckled. 'Hello Ruby.'

'You son of a-'

'Now, now, now!' he said. 'You'll embarrass the books.'

Ruby folded her arms and looked around her, clearly trying to get her temper back under control. Oli had always adored this side of her. Ruby Hutchinson might come across as a sweet little introvert, but he knew all too well what a firecracker she could be.

'You knew it was me all along, didn't you?' she huffed eventually, not meeting his eye.

'I wasn't one hundred per cent sure on the stairs,' said Oli. It was an outright lie, of course, but she'd never know that. 'In my defence, though, I was doing my best not to give birth to my intestines at the time. That stupid trunk weighed a ton. But in the café? Yeah - of course I knew. I mean, I wouldn't have stolen a coffee from a complete stranger, would I? Anyway, there was no mistaking you in that cute little apron.'

The squeak that came from the woman in front of him was probably enough to summon a bunch of bats into the shop. Or dolphins. Dolphins would probably have a harder time navigating the steep high street, though.

'Brings back memories, right?' chuckled Oli, wiggling his eyebrows.

'I'm not doing this with you.'

Oli looked at her and instantly felt bad. He thought she'd been enjoying the joke... at least a little bit. But now all traces of high dudgeon had deserted her, and her voice had come out in a wobbly whisper instead of a snap.

'Rubes - I'm sorry,' he said. 'I didn't-'

'Where's Reuben?' she said, cutting across him.

'Erm... the Cotswolds I think,' said Oli, cocking his head in surprise.

'When's he back?' said Ruby.

'He's... not?' said Oli.

Uh oh... didn't she know...? Surely someone had told her...

'Unless you've invited him to your signing?' he said, hoping that's what she meant. He paused, waiting for her to answer, but Ruby just stood in front of him, her eyes wide. She looked lost, and it was as much as he could do not to reach out and give her a hug.

'He fell in love with a wonderful guy,' said Oli, as soon as he realised she wasn't going to say anything. 'He moved away to be with him.'

'You're not telling me he just left this place behind,' said Ruby quietly. 'There's no way...'

'Well - yeah, he did!' said Oli. 'He sold it to me and danced off into the sunset with his very own romantic hero. From what I've heard on the grapevine, he's really happy. Turns out Rhodders - his beau - is basically landed gentry. We're talking family pile and a huge library.'

'Sounds like Reuben's version of heaven,' she said quietly.

Oli nodded. 'I like to imagine him in his best waistcoat with his feet up in front of the library fire and a book open on his lap.'

Ruby smiled softly for the briefest moment, and Oli felt it knock the breath right out of him.

'So,' she said, clearly trying to pull herself together. 'So... this place is yours now?'

Oli nodded again. 'Didn't your publisher tell you it was me who'd booked you?'

'No,' said Ruby, letting out a long sigh. 'But to be fair to them, that's my fault. When my editor told me I'd be finishing my tour here, she said she'd forward the contact details to me, but I told her not to bother. I told her I knew the owner. I told her we were old friends...'

'Ruby - all those things are still true!' laughed Oli. 'You *do* know the owner, and we *are* old friends.'

'Friends?!' squeaked Ruby.

'You know what I mean,' said Oli tightly. She did

have a point though. *Friends* didn't come anywhere close to describing what they'd been to each other.

'But... but...' spluttered Ruby, taking a tiny step backwards.

'But what?' said Oli, watching her face closely, trying to gauge what was going on in her head.

'But... this means you knew I was coming,' she said, shaking her head in confusion. 'You must have known my team had booked me in here. You *must* have known!' she said again, shooting a glance at the life-sized cut out of herself in the window.

'Known?!' laughed Oli. 'Of course! I was the one who contacted your publishers. I sent the invitation and then convinced them it'd make the perfect end to your tour.' He stopped and ran his fingers through his hair. 'I set up that ridiculous thing in the window, too. Oh - and I bought as many copies of your book as my budget would allow. So yeah - I knew you'd be here.'

Ruby stared at him, looking like he'd just slapped her across the face with a wet haddock. This wasn't right. This wasn't the way he'd planned for this meeting to go.

'Ruby, look-' he started, wanting to go back to the beginning and explain everything.

'I've got to go!'

Before he could even react, Ruby tossed the little key for the collectables cabinet onto the desk, turned on her heel and darted from the shop. The door slamming closed behind her sounded like the most damning full-stop he'd ever heard.

'Well… shit!' he muttered, leaning both hands on his desk. 'That was definitely *not* the plan.'

CHAPTER 7

RUBY

Ruby set off downhill at a trot without even thinking about where she was going. She just wanted to put as much distance between herself and the bookshop as quickly as she could.

Who was she kidding? It wasn't the bookshop she was running away from – it was the unexpected new owner!

The unexpected - still-gorgeous - new owner!

Ruby shook her head and kept marching - past the bakery… the bridal shop… the café. She kept her head down, not daring to peep through any of the windows just in case she locked eyes with someone she knew. She'd already had enough ghosts of the past pop up to greet her for one morning.

Idiot, idiot, idiot!

Ruby had been half dreaming about, half dreading seeing Oli again for more than half a decade. Surely that was more than enough time to figure out exactly what she wanted to say to him when it happened! But *oh* no – he'd taken her by surprise, and in return, she'd done a runner. What was he going to think?!

One thing was for sure – there was no way she was going to be able to set foot back in the bookshop now. Not after making such an epic prat out of herself. Maybe she should just keep marching all the way back to the bottom of town, head straight through the City Gates and catch a lift back to the station. She could go straight back to London and tell her editor the whole thing had fallen through.

It was a tempting thought but…

'Damn it!' she huffed.

In her haste to get away from Oli, she'd managed to storm right out of the bookshop without her bag.

Pausing for the briefest moment, Ruby glanced back up the hill towards the gleaming green and gold frontage. Nope – there was no way she could go back.

A bit like the café, the bookshop had always been a sanctuary - as familiar to her as the back of her own hand. Now, with Reuben gone and Oli in his place, it suddenly felt like alien territory.

He didn't belong in there.
He didn't belong in Crumbleton.
Then again, neither did she.

Ruby knew she was being ridiculous - expecting everything in town to remain unchanged just because she hadn't been here to witness it. Time didn't simply stand still – at least, not for most people. Of *course* things were bound to have changed.

Still, that didn't mean she was happy about it. Crumbleton wasn't meant to change. That was the whole point of the place. It was meant to remain solidly, unshakably the same - a fixed point in her past that she could navigate by – preferably without ever having to return!

Now look what had happened! Reuben was gone and Oli was back. Plus, it had probably happened ages ago – she'd just had no idea. No one had told her - but then, she knew she had no one to blame for that but herself.

Whenever Ruby spoke to her parents, they focused entirely on their own obsessions, with occasional bits of gossip about the university they both worked at thrown in for flavouring. They never mentioned Crumbleton – and Ruby never asked.

What about Caroline, though? Her childhood best friend visited her in London regularly. Caroline also happened to be Oli's cousin, the reason the pair of them had met in the first place, and one of just two people who knew there had ever been anything going on between them beyond their official study-buddy status. How could she have failed to mention the fact not only had he returned from America - but that he'd bought the bookshop too?!

You know why!

The little voice in her head could be annoyingly truthful sometimes.

The only reason she'd managed to stay on such good terms with Caroline was because her friend stuck – rather reluctantly - to her "no news about Crumbleton" rule, as well as the even more important "Oliver Evans *who?!*" rule.

Taking a deep breath, Ruby willed her idiotic heart to calm down and figure out exactly what she should do next. Clearly, her first instinct to run away from Crumbleton forever was a no-go.

'Come on Ruby, you can deal with this!' she muttered, glancing back up the hill and then down again.

She was a successful writer, for goodness sake. She was an adult with a career and… and… and that was where her pep talk came to a grinding halt – just like it always did. Was writing *really* the only thing she had in her life worth mentioning?

Shaking her head, Ruby quickly shoved that particular issue to the back of her brain. Now was definitely *not* the time! First things first – she needed to get off the high street before she did something idiotic like burst into tears. As far as she could see – she had two choices. She could head to her parents' place or go to see Caroline.

Well – there was no way she could face her parents in this state. For one thing, that would mean heading back up the hill towards the bookshop again… and for another, she really didn't want them to know there was anything wrong. Besides, Oli knew where her parents lived – and there was a minuscule chance he might turn up there.

'Hi Ruby! Can't wait for your signing!'

Ruby jumped and then quickly forced herself to return the smile of the man grinning at her as he motored his way up the cobbled street. It was Stuart Bendall, the owner of the shop near the bottom of town that sold everything from groceries to hardware. Luckily, it looked like he was on too much of a mission to stop and chat. He gave her a friendly wave as he strode past.

'Come on idiot,' she muttered, 'time to put the thumb-screws on Caroline!'

She'd go straight to the Crumbleton Times and Echo office for a long-overdue visit. She could really do without any more surprises - and as someone who was actually paid to be nosy, Caroline was the perfect person to fill her in.

Ruby started to head down the hill so fast that the cottages and shops on either side became little more than a cute, pastel-coloured blur. She didn't dare slow down for fear of someone else she knew stopping her in her tracks. Right now, past and present were busy doing a kind of jumbled-up jig inside her head, and she wasn't sure if she wanted to burst into tears or laugh at the absurdity of it all.

There was one thing she was certain of, though -

coming home to Crumbleton had been a spectacularly bad idea. She'd always known it would be the case - but she'd never expected it to be *this* bad!

Taking an abrupt turn to the left, Ruby dashed off the high street and scuttled down a narrow passageway between two cottages. She knew it led to yet another set of stone steps that came out just below the Crumbleton Times and Echo office.

Breathing a sigh of relief to be off the high street for a brief moment, Ruby took the uneven steps two at a time in her haste to see her friend. She knew she was risking more than a twisted ankle right now, but she didn't care.

If she was lucky, maybe she could talk Caroline into grabbing her bag from the bookshop for her. While she was at it, perhaps she'd be kind enough to cancel the signing, apologise to her parents, and then book a taxi back to the train station too…

'Stop being an idiot!' Ruby huffed, ducking her head and nipping beneath a stone archway that led back out onto the high street. She dashed across the road before anyone could see her and straight into the tiny courtyard in front of the newspaper office.

Ruby hammered on the weathered, sage-green door while eyeballing the well-polished brass plaque that read:

Crumbleton Times and Echo.
General Dog's Body: Caroline Cook

Ruby fidgeted. She really needed to get inside before someone spotted her and wanted to talk about the book. Or the old days. Or anything, really.

Shooting a furtive glance behind her, Ruby spotted Iris Tait ambling slowly over the cobbles. Quickly tucking herself in behind a large tree palm in a pot, Ruby held her breath as she peeped through the frondy leaves until Iris was out of sight. Then, without emerging from her hiding place, she stretched out her arm and hammered on the door again.

'I'm coming, I'm coming,' came a familiar voice from inside. 'Hold your horses unless it's the scoop of the century!'

Ruby rolled her eyes and couldn't help smiling as she tried to knock again, only to find her fist bopping around in thin air.

'Ruby Hutchinson, you old baggage!' laughed Caroline. 'What are you trying to do to my pot plant?'

'Use it as camouflage, mostly!' said Ruby, relief flooding through her at the sight of her best friend. 'Can I come in?'

Caroline didn't answer, she just grabbed Ruby's hand and yanked her across the threshold into a bear hug that was so warm and familiar it brought tears to her eyes.

CHAPTER 8

RUBY

'Alright, my old mucker,' said Caroline, thrusting a large glass of water in front of Ruby, 'get that down you, and then tell me what on Earth's got you so worked up!'

Ruby took the glass with trembling fingers and shot her friend a watery smile. She'd known Caroline since they'd both been in nappies... and this was her at her most gentle. As in - not at all. Caroline had always been like a bull in a china shop. It was a trait Ruby found weirdly comforting. Just the fact that there was something as steady and unchangeable as Caroline Cook in Crumbleton made Ruby breathe a sigh of relief.

'Come on Rubes, out with it,' said Caroline, crossing her arms. 'Who do I have to sit on?! Was it your parents?'

Ruby shook her head. 'I've not even seen them yet!'

'Then who?!' demanded Caroline, looking more than a little fierce.

'Oliver. Evans.' Ruby muttered the name between sips of water.

'What's my dear old cuz been doing to reduce you to tears!' said Caroline, her eyes going wide with surprise.

Ruby shook her head and took another sip of water – mainly as a delaying tactic. Perhaps coming to Caroline hadn't been the *best* idea after all. She really wasn't one for tea and sympathy – and Ruby was on the verge of getting hysterical about a guy she hadn't seen since she was a teenager. A guy she'd only dated for one summer. In secret.

'I mean, I know you guys have got the whole *old flame* thing going on,' said Caroline, 'but seriously - it's been years!'

Okay – mostly secret!

Ruby just stared at Caroline, not knowing what to say. How could she admit she was still in love with the same person she'd fallen for all those years ago – when she was just a kid? How could she own up to the fact that she hadn't even dated – let alone had a relationship with anyone – since she'd left Crumbleton?

'Look… are you going to give me the gossip or am I going to have to go snooping?' said Caroline, perching on the edge of her desk and watching Ruby with hawk-like interest.

'Off the record?' said Ruby. It was a force of habit when it came to talking to Caroline.

'It's always off the record with you, Rubes,' laughed Caroline. 'You know that. Unless you explicitly tell me otherwise, of course. Besides, I don't think anyone would be that interested in reading about your teenage exploits… even if you *are* the talk of the town at the moment, what with you being our very own home-grown celeb!'

'Urgh… don't joke!' Ruby wrinkled her nose and shook her head.

'I'm not,' said Caroline in surprise. 'Not about that last bit, at least. You know, I don't understand why you always get your knickers in a twist the moment anyone mentions your writing. You should be proud of what you've achieved! The book is stunning - and by the looks of it, the rest of the world thinks so too. I know we're a bit biased in Crumbleton – but we're allowed to be proud of you, you know!'

Ruby cringed and took another sip of water. How had they just managed to stray from one excruciating topic to another that was equally as painful in a matter of seconds?

'Can we not… with the book stuff?' she said, clearing her throat and glancing up at the intricate mouldings on the ceiling.

Ruby had just come to the annoying realisation that this time, there was no way she could do a runner to avoid talking about a sticky subject. It might have worked with Oli – at least temporarily - but Caroline would probably rugby-tackle her to the cobbles and force answers out of her in the middle of the high street if she tried the same trick on her.

'Why not?' sighed Caroline. 'Come on Rubes… spill!'

'Okay, fine' said Ruby, quickly deciding that out of the two topics on the table - Oli or writing - writing was *marginally* less puke-worthy. 'I liked the writing bit… when it was just me, in my bedroom - and the characters were talking to me and all I had to do was bung everything on a page.' She paused and glanced at Caroline, but her friend stayed quiet. 'Then I finished it and sent it out… because that's what you're meant to do, right?'

Caroline shrugged and nodded.

'And then the world went mad. It felt like I blinked and suddenly I had this agent. Blink again and I had a publisher and an editor who believed in the story.'

'But surely that's a good thing?' said Caroline. 'Kind of the whole point?'

'Yeah,' said Ruby nodding. 'Harriet wanted the book to be as strong as it could be. Her edits were brilliant - but every change I made took me one step further away from the story I'd cosied up with on my own for so long.'

'Weird process!' said Caroline.

Ruby nodded again. She knew she sounded ridiculous right now - that's why she never talked about this to anyone. But this wasn't just *anyone...* this was Caroline. She knew she could talk to her about pretty much anything.

'I know I'm lucky,' she said grudgingly. 'Plenty of people have made it blindingly obvious that this is the kind of thing other writers would give a kidney for.'

'Right,' said Caroline. 'I mean… maybe not an actual body-part… but…'

'You know what I mean!' Ruby huffed at her ever-literal friend. 'Anyway – before I knew what was happening, there were all these international auctions… and… well… suddenly I'm getting all this attention for this book and it doesn't feel right. I don't deserve all this fuss.'

'Why not,' laughed Caroline. 'You wrote it!'

'I did… but I don't really remember much about it. I just sat down and hammered it out. Harriet's edits were what polished it. Now everyone wants me to talk about writing the blasted thing until the cows come home.'

'Okay – breathe!' said Caroline, sounding unusually gentle. 'You're at the end of a pretty long tour. It's natural you're a bit tired of the whole thing and bored of the same old questions.'

'But I've felt like this from the very first interview,' said Ruby. 'And now Harriet's dropping hints about the next book!'

'Well… that's a good thing too,' said Caroline. 'You can hole back up in your flat, pretend the world doesn't exist, and get back to the bit you *did* enjoy about the whole process.'

'It won't be the same,' said Ruby, feeling a wave of exhaustion roll over her.

'Why on Earth not?!' said Caroline.

'Because now I know what happens when I'm done with it. I know I'll have to jump straight back on this marketing treadmill.' She paused, gnawing at her lip until she tasted the metallic tang of blood. 'There'll be more deadlines. More pressure…'

'More sales, more money,' countered Caroline. 'What an amazing life!'

'That's just it!' Ruby practically shouted in frustration.

'*What's* just it?' said Caroline. Her voice was still calm and low, but she held Ruby's eyes with the kind of intensity that demanded the truth.

'I don't have a life,' muttered Ruby. 'No real friends, no community. I'm not at home anywhere.'

'Excuse me?' huffed Caroline, suddenly looking decidedly put out. 'You *have* friends. You've *always* had friends. It's not our fault you absolutely refuse to come home to see us.'

'I didn't mean…' said Ruby quickly. 'I just meant… not up there. Not in London.'

'Then why are you still living there?' said Caroline. 'Why is this the first time I've seen you home in six years? Why is it that - whenever I need my Ruby fix - I have to shlep all the way to the bloody capital?'

Silence descended on the room for a long moment, and it was as much as Ruby could do not to make a break for the door.

'Well... at least you're here now I guess,' said Caroline, after the moment had stretched out so far it felt like it was going to snap.

'I'm only here because I had to come back,' Ruby muttered. 'Trust me, I'll be out of here the minute I've signed the last book... if not before.'

'Wait... what?' said Caroline, looking hurt. 'I thought you'd at least stay for a couple of weeks!'

'It wasn't my idea to come back, you know,' said Ruby. 'It was Harriet's - and there was no talking her out of it. Believe me – I tried. But then I figured at least I'd get to see you, and my parents, and Reuben-'

'But Reuben moved away more than a year ago!' said Caroline, looking confused.

'Well, I know that now!' huffed Ruby. 'The bookshop belongs to-'

'Oli,' said Caroline, nodding.

'Why didn't you tell me?!' demanded Ruby.

'I assumed you knew!' said Caroline with a little laugh. 'I mean... you *are* doing an event for him in a couple of days. And he chased that *hard.*'

'No he didn't,' scoffed Ruby. 'Harriet chased that hard.'

'Have it your way,' said Caroline mildly, standing up and making her way around to her chair on the other side of the desk. 'Anyway – you can't blame me for not filling you in. I couldn't tell you anything about him, could I?'

'But-' said Ruby

'After he left for America,' said Caroline, raising her voice to cut across her, 'you made me swear I'd never - *ever* - mention my cousin to you again. Ever. On pain of-'

'Disembowelment,' said Ruby quietly. Because she *had* said that. She leaned forward and dropped her head into her hands. 'Car,' she breathed, 'I'm… I'm sorry for being such a selfish ass.'

'You're not an ass!' said Caroline.

'But I have been selfish,' countered Ruby.

'To be fair, Rubes, you were just trying to find your way in the world like the rest of us,' said Caroline. 'But I always thought, when you'd had a break from Crumbleton's slightly smothering embrace – and got over the thing with Oli - you'd come back. At least for a visit.'

Ruby looked up again and pulled a face.

'Was it *really* that bad here?' said Caroline. 'I thought we had a pretty awesome childhood! I thought you were happy. I mean… I just don't understand. Please don't tell me I missed some deep, dark secret about my closest friend that completely effed you up!'

Ruby stared at Caroline, not daring to blink.

'Shit,' breathed Caroline. 'There *was* something. This isn't just a random break from Crumbleton that got out of hand…'

Ruby gave her head the slightest of shakes. 'I couldn't stay here after Oli left,' she said. 'There were just too many memories…'

'But *you* were the one who stopped contacting *him*!' said Caroline. 'How come-'

'I had to!' said Ruby. 'I didn't have a choice!'

'But… why?' said Caroline. 'I mean – he got on that plane and then cut him out of your life. Hell – you even took yourself off social media – who does that?!'

'I didn't have a choice,' she said again. 'Oli's dad…'

'Uncle Mike?' said Caroline with a frown.

Ruby nodded. 'I guess he was just doing what he thought was best for Oli. I don't know how he found out about us – but he came into the café one day when I was working. It was early and I was on my own out front.'

'What did he say?' said Caroline, her eyes wide.

If you really love him, you'll let him go. If you really love him, you'll disappear and make sure he gets the life he deserves. But you don't love him, do you? You don't even care - because you're going to let him throw everything away for you.

Ruby shrugged. Caroline didn't need to know what a git her uncle was. At least – not the specifics.

'He just said I'd be holding Oli back if I didn't let him go,' she said, swallowing a hard lump of emotion.

'I hate to speak ill of the dead,' sighed Caroline, 'but the guy was always a bit of an arse.'

'Oli's dad's dead?' said Ruby, feeling the shock hit her in the chest like a physical blow.

Caroline nodded.

'Wait – is that why Oli came back?' said Ruby.

'No, I don't think so,' said Caroline.

'Then why-'

'You know,' said Caroline, 'I think you two really need to talk to *each other* about this. As much as I adore playing piggy-in-the-middle...'

'Wait – has Oli said something to you about me?' said Ruby.

Caroline let out a long sigh. '*You* might have banned me from ever mentioning his name, but my darling cousin never made the same demand about you - sadly!'

'Tell me what he said!' said Ruby.

'No chance,' said Caroline.

'But why?' said Ruby, wide-eyed. 'Was it bad? Wait... maybe I don't want to know.'

Caroline snorted. 'Look, why don't you head up to your parents' place and chill out for a bit. Unpack, get settled, and then you can go back to the bookshop for a proper catch-up with him.'

'Can't,' said Ruby.

'Why on Earth not?' said Caroline.

'I kind of stormed out when I discovered that he was the new owner... and left my bag behind,' she said, feeling her face flush.

'Well then – you'll just have to go back there first,' said Caroline with an easy shrug.

'That'd be a bit inconvenient, considering I've vowed never to set foot in the place ever again,' she huffed.

'My goodness - you *are* a drama queen!' chuckled Caroline.

'It's not funny!' said Ruby.

'It's flippin' hilarious!' said Caroline stoutly. 'Let me lay it out for you. One,' she held up a finger, 'just the idea we'll be able to keep you out of any bookshop is laughable. Two,' a second finger went up, 'you have an event in there the day after tomorrow. You've always been a good girl - so you'll be there. And three,' Caroline held up a third finger, 'you and my cousin - who I've heard members of the local WI describe as "our beautiful beefy bookseller" - clearly have things you need to talk about.'

'I… no… we…' spluttered Ruby.

'That's what I thought,' said Caroline. 'I think six years is plenty long enough for both of you to stew, don't you?'

'I think I'll go see my parents now,' said Ruby quietly.

'Wuss!' chuckled Caroline. 'But yeah, you better had. Erm… one question, though-'

'Just the one?' said Ruby, hauling herself to her feet. She was exhausted. She might have only just got back, but she felt like she'd gone ten rounds with the little town already.

'Yeah, for now,' said Caroline. 'What are you going to do about your bag?'

'Erm…' Ruby ran her fingers through her hair. 'Maybe… I was wondering… could you…?'

'Double wuss!' chuckled Caroline. 'But fine - you go put your poor parents out of their misery. I know they're a bit nutty - but they do love you - and I bet they've missed you.'

'Deep down,' muttered Ruby.

'Well, yeah,' said Caroline. 'I've got to go up to the museum a bit later anyway, so I'll nip into the bookshop and grab your bag on the way.'

'You will?' said Ruby.

'Of course,' said Caroline. 'You know I'd do anything for you… and besides, it'll give me a chance to get the low-down on how Oli feels about you being back in town.'

'You wouldn't dare?!' said Ruby, her eyes going wide.

'Oh come on Rubes!' said Caroline, a decidedly naughty twinkle in her eye. 'He's back in town… and single. You're back in town… and single… Just think of the possibilities!'

'Nope. No no no,' said Ruby, shaking her head. 'No possibilities,' she added firmly, even though something at the back of her brain seemed to be shifting - rearranging itself around this new bit of information.

It wasn't that she'd never wondered about Oli's relationship status, but she'd never dreamed of actually trying to find out.

'No,' she said again, more firmly. 'I'm here for all of five minutes - then I'm gone. I don't need you stirring things up.'

'Spoilsport,' pouted Caroline. 'Well, I'll grab your bag - but at least let me just *double-check* that Oli doesn't have anyone else in the picture.'

'Yes please to the bag,' said Ruby grudgingly. 'As to any digging, that's nothing to do with me.'

'Oh come on, admit it. You want all the gossip about my idiot cousin!' said Caroline with a grin.

'Fine. I do,' sighed Ruby. 'But don't mention me… and just make sure it's-'

'Yeah, yeah, off the record,' said Caroline, rolling her eyes.

CHAPTER 9

OLI

Pushing himself up off the counter – where he'd spent the last ten minutes with his head in his hands - Oli scrubbed at his face and stared around the shop.

How had that just gone so spectacularly wrong?

He'd always known that inviting Ruby Hutchinson to do an event at the bookshop was a huge risk – both business and personal. For one thing, she hadn't set foot in town since he'd moved to America – a fact that Caroline had rather grumpily verified on numerous occasions. For another – he wasn't entirely sure how she'd feel about the fact that he'd bought the bookshop from Reuben.

He'd turned these things over and over in his mind for days before approaching her publisher – adding in his worries about their history together – but eventually, he'd decided to go ahead and do it anyway. Oli had been more than prepared for Ruby to turn the whole thing down flat, so it had been a wonderful surprise when her publisher had been downright excited about the idea of her finishing off the tour in her hometown.

According to them, the whole team was on board – Crumbleton Bookshop would be the perfect final stop for their new star author. All they had to do was get her to agree. Which she did. Eventually.

Oli had been bouncing between nervous, excited, hopeful and shocked ever since. He couldn't quite believe Ruby had agreed to it!

'It all makes sense now, though,' he sighed.

Ruby hadn't agreed to come to *his* shop after all. She'd thought she was teaming up with Reuben. Hell, she hadn't even expected to find him back in town.

'Gah!' he grunted, getting to his feet and pacing to the other side of the shop, where he stopped and eyeballed the dozens of copies of *Every Little Dream* that were stacked up neatly, ready for her signature.

Picking one up, he flipped it over and stared at the author photograph on the back cover – just as he'd done about a thousand times already.

This picture was what had convinced him that it would be safe for him to see her again. It looked nothing like the Ruby Hutchinson he remembered – the bookworm who'd helped him drag his English grade up far enough for him to win his coveted sports scholarship. *That* Ruby had turned out to be funny, feisty and so incredibly kind that Oli had fallen head-over-heels for her the first time they'd faced each other over his study notes. A complication his father *definitely* hadn't seen coming when he'd suggested private tutoring.

It hadn't taken long before their study sessions – long evenings and weekends pouring over Jane Austen's Persuasion and endless pages of Shakespeare - became Oli's favourite time of the week. He loved spending time with Ruby, but he hadn't been expecting to fall for the subject too. There was something about the way Ruby approached books - and reading - that made him see it differently. It came to life under her gentle touch… a bit like he did too.

By the time Oli sat his exams, he was cheating on sports with English Lit. In fact, the lure of the track and field scholarship – something he'd been working towards for years – had lost all its charm. When Oli announced that he didn't want to go to America after all - that he wanted to study English at a British university instead – his dad had taken matters into his own hands.

'And the rest, as they say, is history,' muttered Oli.

As usual, his dad had got his own way. Oli won his scholarship and went to America. He'd "run track" as they'd called it over there. He'd even had a shot at competing in the Olympics. He'd done it all with a broken heart – because the minute he boarded that plane, Ruby had disappeared from his life.

Oli let out a long sigh. Rehashing the past was pointless. His dad was gone now – but at least he'd tried to put things right first – and at least Oli had had the chance to say goodbye.

Now, armed with that truth and a reason to finally draw Ruby back to Crumbleton, maybe there was a chance to… to…

To what? Make her fall back in love with him? Convince a talented, celebrated author that she could love a small-town bookseller who'd once had his own shot at stardom and walked away from it?

'You're an idiot!' said Oli.

It had all backfired so spectacularly. She'd looked so horrified to see him. He'd never wanted her to feel like she'd been tricked into coming back. He'd wanted it to be her choice!

Oli stared at the author photograph again, searching Ruby's eyes as though he might find an answer there. It didn't help. It really didn't look like her. The woman he'd come face-to-face just now hadn't changed a jot, though. Other than looking a bit tired and freaked out, she was as gorgeous as she'd always been.

'And then you made her run away!' he muttered.

Oli could kick himself for joking around with her

like that in the café. He'd thought it would be funny – but in his defence, he'd thought she was in on the joke! How come Caroline hadn't told her that he'd bought the bookshop?! The pair of them had been friends forever.

It wasn't his cousin's fault, though. She'd warned him years ago that Ruby had flat-out banned her from even mentioning his name. She'd put up so many barriers that she basically lived in a Crumbleton-free fortress. A fortress Oli had been well and truly locked out of.

Oli sighed and carefully placed the book back down onto the top of the pile, wondering if they'd ever see her signature now. In fact... that was something he *really* needed to find out! Maybe he should call her publicity team. Maybe he should-

Oli's eyes landed on the patchwork armchair... and the large rucksack leaning against it.

Ruby's bag! She must have forgotten it in her hurry to get away from him.

Dashing to the door, he wrenched it open and stepped out onto the high street, staring first up the hill and then down. He spotted Stuart from Bendall's nipping into the café, and further down the hill, he could just see Iris Tait tugging her wheeled trolly over the cobbles. But there was no sign of Ruby.

Heading back inside the shop, Oli shut the door behind him and flipped the sign to "Closed" – popping the little "back in 10 minutes" card he kept handy just below it.

Then he headed over to the counter, grabbed a sheet of paper from the printer tray, and picked up a pen.

Dear Ruby...

CHAPTER 10

RUBY

The minute she was back out on the high street, Ruby decided that she couldn't be bothered with any more shortcuts. There wasn't much point sneaking around now that her worst nightmare had already come true, was there?

Drama queen!

Caroline's words echoed in her head, and she broke into a grin. Perhaps her friend was right.

Tying her jumper around her waist, Ruby route-marched up the cobbles, nodding and smiling at the various locals who greeted her as she went. After all – she might as well get used to it. Caroline had made her promise that she wouldn't pull a disappearing act before the pair of them had had the chance for a longer catch-up – preferably with a stiff drink in front of them.

It didn't take her long to reach the entrance to the

little alleyway that led to her parents' house. As she turned off the high street and made her way between the two ancient buildings, Ruby's steps faltered. She was nervous. Perhaps it would have been a better idea to grab herself a room down at the Dolphin and Anchor instead of asking her parents if she could stay in her childhood bedroom. After such a long time away, she wasn't sure how she was going to feel about being back.

Coming to a halt in front of the peeling, dark red front door, Ruby smiled ruefully to herself. Her mum might not exactly be your typical parent… but even *she* might have something to say about her only daughter staying somewhere else on her first visit home in six years!

Taking a deep breath, Ruby did her best to steady her nerves and prepare herself for what was waiting inside. Her parents – and reminders of her childhood around every corner. Or… maybe not. They might have renovated the entire place for all she knew.

Ruby stared up at the crooked lines of the old house. It was about three hundred years old, and the building leaned slightly to one side, as if it was starting to feel its age and would really quite like to sit down. The window frames weren't exactly square, and it definitely needed a bit of TLC - but there was something comforting about its familiarity.

'Okay, here we go,' she muttered, lifting the latch to let herself in.

Of course, this door didn't lead directly into the house itself. The "front door" was actually a great big faker. It led to a hidden passageway which scooted right through the middle of the house to the back.

Ruby made her way along it, squeezing past a pile of firewood and her dad's bike, until she reached a tiny courtyard garden. She was about to let herself through the back door into the kitchen when a voice made her turn.

'There you are!'

Her mother's smiling, *very* grubby face popped up from beside the one and only flower bed. Ruby couldn't understand how she hadn't spotted her, considering there wasn't much to the little garden – just the bed, a patch of grass, and a few shrubs all hemmed in by the craggy stone walls of neighbouring houses on the hill.

The garden had never really been given the care and attention it deserved – considering neither Ruby nor her parents had much interest in gardening. In fact, it was quite disconcerting to find her mum out there now - especially considering she was leaning on a spade!

'Mum!' said Ruby, smiling as a syrupy puddle of pure love bubbled up inside her. 'What on *earth* are you up to? Earth being the operative word here!' Ruby nodded at the scruffy patch of lawn – which was even scruffier than usual. It looked like a demented rabbit had been having a field day.

'What do you think this is?' said her mum, completely ignoring Ruby's question and bending down to retrieve something from a pile of other… somethings…

'I truly have no idea!' said Ruby, completely nonplussed.

'Hmm…' she said, staring at the thing in her hand. 'I'm not sure it's the one. I'm not even sure if I'm holding the blasted thing the right way up!' She tossed it back onto the pile and beamed at Ruby.

'Erm… "the one" for what?!' said Ruby, doing her best to catch up.

'The one to win the Odd Object Competition at the museum, of course!' said her mum as though she was being deliberately slow to cotton on. 'That trophy's mine this year! Iris Tait reckons she's going to win again, but I bet she's going to go with that stupid thing that looks like a miniature cheese grater again. She entered that in 1992 - and that's against the rules.'

Ruby smirked. She felt a bit like she'd climbed inside a time machine. Nothing had changed… she could have just come home from school. She wasn't sure what she'd been expecting after such a long time away - maybe a hug or a bit of a fuss… maybe being dragged inside for a cuppa. She definitely hadn't been expecting a distracted conversation over a pile of unidentified objects in the back garden!

'Your dad's inside somewhere,' said her mum, turning back to the flower bed and thrusting her spade into a fresh spot. 'He's meant to be fixing the washing machine.'

And that was that. Ruby knew better than to expect anything else out of her mum while she was hyper-focussed on a task – no matter how random! She shrugged and headed for the back door. She'd go and say hi to her dad, and then head upstairs to her room. She had to admit, she was really dreading that bit.

Other than checking with her parents that it would be okay for her to stay with them - and making sure there was still a bed in her room - Ruby hadn't dared to ask if they'd done anything else with it. Not that she'd blame them if they had, of course - six years was a long time. They might have turned it into an office... or a gym.

Grinning at the idea of either of her bookish parents on an elliptical, Ruby gave the crooked door a good push and then stepped back in time into her childhood.

The kitchen was exactly as she remembered it. It smelled of warm, fresh bread with an underlying note of coffee. The pine table in the centre of the room was heaped with all sorts - from books and piles of receipts to a bowl of slightly wizened grapes and what looked like a cardboard model of a rocket ship.

Ruby glanced around for her dad, but he was nowhere to be seen. The washing machine had been pulled out from its usual hiding place underneath the counter, and there was a toolbox abandoned in front of it.

A warm sense of familiarity and comfort wrapped its arms around Ruby and she sighed. She'd really not expected to feel like this.

'Ruby Ruby Ruby!' cheered her dad, appearing in the low, sagging doorway that led through to the rest of the house.

'Dad!'

He mooched over to her and gave her a bristly kiss on the cheek before heading for the washing machine. 'I'd give you a hug,' he said, 'but I'm filthy!'

Ruby grinned, noting that he had his red overalls on - a sure sign that her mum had put him to work on household chores for the day. It was the only time he ever wore them.

'What are you up to?' she said lightly, watching him fiddling around with the plug for the ancient machine.

'Making a start on my to-do list,' he chuckled, half nodding at the door to the airing cupboard.

Ruby turned to it. Her mum had covered it with blackboard paint back when she'd been in primary school - and it had been the official household calendar and to-do list ever since. Sure enough, its surface was covered in white chalk - her mum's spidery scrawl detailing a long list of jobs. Right at the top - underneath the title "Things to Fix Before Ruby Comes Home" were the words "Fix Washing Machine."

'So… how's that coming on?' she said, turning back to her dad.

He shrugged, popped a new fuse into the plug and then quickly screwed it back together. 'Let's see, shall we?' he said, shoving it back into the socket. 'If this doesn't go pop or trip the board, I'd say we're onto a winner!'

Ruby braced herself as he flipped the switch and hit the big "on" button on the ancient machine.

Water instantly started to rattle through the pipes and pour into the drum - and her dad executed a triumphant fist pump. 'One down!'

'And about twenty million to go!' said Ruby, glancing at the list again.

'Right!' said her dad, bending down and grabbing a large hammer from his toolbox. 'I'm on a roll.'

With that, he disappeared off towards the living room at the back of the house without another word.

Ruby raised her eyebrows. 'Welcome home, Ruby,' she muttered. 'We know this must be weird for you. Let me make you a cup of tea and let's talk about why you've avoided your childhood home for more than half a decade!'

She sighed. Why *should* they dance around her just because she'd been an idiot about something that had happened so long ago?!

'What was that?' said her dad, his head reappearing at the doorway, making her jump.

'Nothing, dad!' she said, smiling sweetly. 'I was just

mumbling to myself about having to get my bag... I erm left it at-'

'The bookshop! I *knew* there was something I was meant to tell you!' he said, slapping his leg. 'It's upstairs on your bed. Arrived about five minutes before you did.'

Ruby was just wondering how Caroline had managed to dash to the bookshop, subject Oli to the third degree *and* deliver her bag in such a short time when her dad wandered off again.

'Always did like that boy.'

The words drifted back to her, and Ruby felt her spine stiffen.

'*What* boy?' she called after him. 'WHAT BOY?'

It was no use. Her dad was already getting to work on something with his hammer, and the only answer she got was a series of several loud bangs. Still, it wasn't like she really needed an answer, was it? Ruby knew precisely *what boy!*

CHAPTER 11

RUBY

*R*uby darted out of the kitchen and took the narrow, slightly crooked stairs two at a time as she made for her childhood bedroom.

She might have been dreading this moment, but she didn't even pause before flinging the door open. She barely even registered the coating of bookish stickers still present on its once-glossy surface. Right now, the question as to whether Oliver Evans had been up here just minutes ago trumped everything else.

Her eyes flew to the bed. Sure enough, sitting on top of the soft quilt her grandma had sewn for her sixth birthday, was her rucksack.

'Oh noooo!' she groaned. Ruby's insides felt like they'd somehow just melted.

It was a kind, thoughtful thing to do… but she didn't want Oli to be kind and thoughtful. She didn't want him to be anything. She *definitely* didn't want him to be here in Crumbleton.

Keeping a respectful distance between herself and the bag, Ruby slumped down onto the bed. Then she stiffened as she imagined Oli himself sitting right where she was. Had he been here in her room? Had he brought the bag up himself - or just left it downstairs with her dad?

Ruby sniffed the air as though the answer might be lingering in a waft of manly scent - that mix of old books combined with something deep and woody she'd caught earlier in the bookshop.

'Pull yourself together!' she muttered, shooting a glance at her bag out of the corner of her eye, as though not making proper eye contact with it might mean it wasn't really there.

'Wait… what?!'

Something white caught her eye. A piece of folded printer paper lay on the quilt just behind her bag. Ruby reached out for it with tentative fingers, half expecting it to bite. Of course - it didn't, it was just a piece of paper.

Unfolding it slowly, Ruby instantly recognised the tight, loopy scrawl from years ago. Memories flooded back – of nervous knots twisting in her stomach as she prepared to help the most popular boy in the whole school - the star of the sports field - to study for his English literature exams.

Ruby stared at the note, not reading the words but letting her eyes drift down to the signature at the bottom. Oli E. There it was, along with a great big kiss.

'Oh shit,' she sighed, folding the paper up again – over and over until it was in a tight little wad. She was more than a little bit tempted to bung it straight in the bin. Instead, she thrust it into her jeans pocket.

Out of sight, out of mind.

Coming home to Crumbleton was always going to be tough, but now that Oli was here too, it had reached a whole other level. Clambering to her feet, Ruby took a deep breath as she hunted for any kind of distraction. She stared around her old bedroom. The result was an instant lump in her throat and the sensation of an elephant sitting on her chest.

Not a single thing had changed.

Across the room, under the window that looked out onto Crumbleton High Street, sat her desk. She might have had all the freedom in the world as a kid… but the reality was - she'd been a good girl who'd craved nothing but her parents' attention and approval. When the first wasn't forthcoming, and the second was only granted with a kind of dithery detachment, Ruby had turned to schoolwork and lost herself in writing.

The old Royal typewriter she'd bought with her pocket money at ten years old was sitting exactly where she'd left it - a page of slightly yellowed paper still wound in place.

Ruby frowned. She could just make out a single line of type. Moving closer, she peered at the words.

I have to leave this place. Without him, it's just-

She'd never finished the sentence.

'...just not home,' she whispered.

But now, the *him* in question was back.

With one swift movement, she yanked the paper out of the old typewriter, crumpled it into a tight ball and lobbed it at the waste paper basket. The room may have sat untouched for years - save for some cursory hoovering - but she couldn't bear the idea of leaving that unfinished sentence hanging around a minute longer.

Breathing heavily, Ruby made a slow turn on the spot as her teenage years came to life around her. There were drawings all over the walls. Scrappy sketches of her favourite people and places around the town. Stacks of notebooks leaned drunkenly against teetering piles of typewritten pages next to her desk. They contained millions of words - hundreds of stories and ideas - all featuring people who'd surrounded her in her day-to-day life. Ruby shuddered. The old feeling of being hemmed in was starting to creep over her.

It was the exact feeling Oli had saved her from all those years ago.

Turning back to the bed, Ruby tossed her bag onto the floor and collapsed onto the mattress. The resulting cloud of dust made her nose tickle, and she sneezed.

'Just read the damn note!' she growled.

Yanking it back out of her pocket before she could change her mind again, Ruby unfolded the page and smoothed out the creases. She'd just have to ignore the fact that her hands were shaking so much the whole thing was quivering.

Dear Ruby,
You left your bag in the shop. I thought you might need it, so I'm going to drop it off with your mum and dad - I guess that's where you're staying?
We need to talk about your event. I was hoping to go over it earlier, but I guess it was all a bit much and you needed to - land a bit? Anyway, I'll be down at the Dolphin & Anchor this evening at 7pm. I'll grab a quiet table. I want to make sure I've got everything you need lined up. Tickets have sold out, so we should have a good crowd.
Here's my mobile number in case you need it. See you later.
Or not.
I'll be there either way.
Oli E x

Ruby stared for several long minutes at the kiss after his name before letting her eyes drift to the carefully printed phone number below.

This doesn't mean anything. Nothing at all.

Except… it did. After six years of maintaining zero contact - six years of avoiding social media like the plague - she had his phone number in her hands.

'It doesn't mean a thing,' she huffed, trying to convince herself

Caroline might have said he was single - but that didn't mean he was remotely interested in her other than as a visiting author. Just because *her* life had been on hold ever since she'd left Crumbleton - ever since *he'd* left Crumbleton - it didn't mean the same thing was true for him.

'Not your *whole* life,' she muttered, coming to her own defence. She might have avoided any kind of personal life, but she'd thrown herself into her writing. She had a career. A successful one.

Write edit submit. Write edit submit. Late nights and early mornings, filling page after page with words until she got the deal. Then her lonely life exploded with meetings, edits, tours and readings.

But now... Oli was here... and she was going to have to face him.

'Maybe not tonight,' she whispered.

After all, what would her parents say if she deserted them on her first night home?! The thought made Ruby snort in amusement. As excuses went, it was a lame one. If she was being honest, they probably wouldn't even notice if she went out.

Ruby had spent quite a bit of her childhood wishing she had more "normal" parents – but they'd always done things their own way. They encouraged independence – developing self-sufficiency and spending time on interests. They chased their own with zeal and urged her to do the same.

The three of them had lived in this house more like roommates than a family. In one way, it had given her so much freedom… but in another, Ruby just wanted to be able to turn to them about all the usual things. Like boys and broken hearts.

'Get me out of here!' she sighed.

She should have put her foot down and told her publisher that Crumbleton was out of the question. But… here she was. Always the good girl - save for that wonderful, brief interlude that had changed the course of her life forever.

Ruby stared at Oli's note again, letting her eyes linger on every little loop, tail and dot… and then those numbers. She should grab her mobile and call him right now. She should tell him that she wasn't going to be at the Dolphin and Anchor. She should tell him that she wasn't even going to be at the signing.

'Of course you will,' huffed Ruby, turning over and burying her face in the musty pillows.

Of course she would. Because she was *still* a good girl… and because, after all these years, she still craved his company. He was like a drug she'd gone cold turkey on – and she didn't have the strength to stay away from him any longer. Not when she had so many ready-made excuses not to.

A knock at the door made Ruby sit bolt upright.

'Yep?' she squeaked, scared that she'd somehow managed to summon him to her door just by thinking about him too much.

'Rubes – your dad's off to the chippy over at Crumbleton Sands later to bring back some tea. You want something?'

It was her mum. This was the way it had always been. No family meals... just a kind of free-for-all student set-up.

'No ta,' she said, keeping her voice as light as possible. 'I've got to meet Oli later to talk about the signing.'

'Oh – exciting...' said her mum.

Ruby held her breath. She wanted to ask if her parents were planning to be there... but she didn't dare. Mainly because her heart would break a tiny bit if the answer was *no* – even if it wouldn't really be a surprise.

'See you later, then,' said her mum.

'Yeah,' sighed Ruby, 'see you.'

Blinking hard and telling herself not to be an idiot, Ruby grabbed her phone. She wasn't going to text Oli - she'd just turn up. At least that way she could back out at the last minute if she needed to.

Instead, she pulled up Caroline's number.

Don't worry about the bag. According to the parentals, Oli dropped it over before I got back. He asked me to meet him later at the D&A. What should I do?

She kind of hated the fact that she'd been back all of three seconds and was already deferring to her friend rather than making adult decisions for herself. But still... she needed backup on this particular conundrum.

Go! What have you got to lose?

Ruby cocked her head. It was a good question. Not much other than her dignity - and frankly that was in shreds already.

Kinda excited and dreading it at the same time

She sent the message without thinking about it too much. Two seconds later, her phone vibrated.

Love is in the air!

Ruby's eyes widened. Nope nope nope. She really didn't need Caroline saying stupid stuff like that - even if it was just to her. After all, this was Crumbleton. The walls had ears!

All business. Anything else is ancient history that NO ONE needs to be talking about!

Ruby hauled herself off the bed. She needed to find something to wear that hadn't faced several hours on a train followed by far too much dashing up and down the hill. She'd only just managed to yank the backpack open when her phone vibrated again.

Spoilsport.

CHAPTER 12

OLI

'You need a hand there, Boss?'

Oli had just tried – and failed – to get through the doorway of the Dolphin and Anchor. He looked up to find Kendra, his Saturday girl, staring at him

'Actually – yes please!' he laughed, feeling like an idiot. 'I'm… stuck!'

He really should have made two trips instead of opening the door with his butt while hefting a heavy picnic basket in one hand and trying to keep a jug full of a dozen yellow roses from slipping out of the other. He'd thought he'd just about got away with it when something caught on the door handle and he'd bounced backwards like he was attached to a bungee cord. The resulting crash had made every single person in the bar turn towards him – local and tourist alike.

'Here!' said Kendra, dashing towards him and taking the roses before they ended up on the floor.

'Cheers!' he said, squirming on the spot. 'Erm... I think I'm attached to the door!'

Kendra placed the roses on the nearest table and then quickly got to work on unhooking his jumper from the handle. He had to hand it to her – she was just about managing to keep a straight face – no mean feat for the fun-loving eighteen-year-old. He had a feeling she wouldn't let him live this down any time soon, though. He was already dreading the weekend!

Kendra worked at the bookshop every Saturday - but Oli wasn't the only person in Crumbleton she called "Boss". Her easy-going nature and willingness to help meant that she was in high demand and had about four different jobs. She was a hard worker, reliable and ridiculously popular - with the local businesses and their customers alike.

'Thanks!' said Oli as soon as she'd managed to free him from the door. His face was hot and he did his best not to meet Kendra's eye. She was busy making a valiant attempt not to giggle. 'Erm – would you mind bringing the flowers over to the table? I'm not sure I trust myself not to cause more havoc!'

'Sure,' said Kendra, with a grin. 'Brilliant entrance there, by the way... very smooth!'

'Oh hush!' muttered Oli, returning her smile.

Kendra grabbed the jug of flowers and gave them a

deep sniff. 'Blimey boss – these are proper fancy. You didn't have to, you know!'

'*Not* for you,' he chuckled.

Why did Oli suddenly get the feeling he was going to regret his choice of venue? Asking Ruby to meet him at the Dolphin and Anchor was never going to afford them any privacy - but he'd hoped it might help her feel a bit more comfortable than inviting her back to his little flat above the shop. What he hadn't banked on was Kendra being behind the bar.

The girl in question was now ushering him past a line of locals nursing their pints at the bar, towards a little table set for two. Oli breathed a sigh of relief when he saw that it was in a relatively quiet corner, underneath the dartboard. They'd have to move if Brian Singer turned up for a game against himself, but as far as Oli could remember – that wasn't due to happen until tomorrow night.

'So, who's the mystery woman?' said Kendra in excitement, watching as Oli plonked the basket onto the table and then slid into one of the chairs. 'Actually – don't answer that. I love a good bit of suspense mixed in with my romance… there's nothing like a real-life rom-com coming to life in front of my very eyes.'

'Wow – you read too much!' muttered Oli, shooting a quick glance towards the door to double-check that Ruby hadn't appeared yet. He really didn't need her overhearing the term "rom-com" right now – it was clear she was already a flight risk!

'As the town's bookseller, that's possibly your worst line ever,' said Kendra, looking mildly affronted.

'Yeah – okay – good point!' said Oli. 'And you know I'd never mean it, right? Sorry to disappoint you though, but this is just a business meeting.'

'Yeah, riiiiiight!' she smirked, looking pointedly at the flowers again. 'What are these about, then?'

'A nice gesture for a visiting author,' said Oli tightly, sliding the jug across the table so they were slightly less prominent.

'Visiting author?' said Kendra.

Her usually low, sultry voice had just risen to a squeak, and Oli glanced up at her only to find that she was practically bouncing with excitement.

'Kendra…' started Oli, a warning note in his voice.

'Are you… are you talking about Ruby Hutchinson?' she breathed.

'Yes,' sighed Oli. There was no point denying it considering she'd *hopefully* be here in the next few minutes.

Oli bit his lip. This was quite possibly the worst idea he'd ever had. His Saturday girl was *obsessed* with Ruby. He could understand it – Kendra was a die-hard bookworm and Ruby's debut was, quite frankly, stunning. But - he was still having a hard time reconciling funny, sweet, slightly shy Ruby he'd known all those years ago with the genius who'd written the book. It wasn't a surprise to discover she had so much talent – it just wasn't the first thing that popped into his head when he let himself think about Ruby.

No - the first thing you think about is her smile, her laugh, her lips – and what it was like to kiss them!

Oli shook his head, hoping it might dislodge the rogue thought and send it packing. He needed to keep his head on straight – otherwise, he risked screwing things up even further.

'Do you think she'll sign something for me?' said Kendra, looking frantic. 'I don't have my book with me but... maybe she'll sign my bag? Or my arm? Or... maybe I could run home real quick and grab-'

'I'm sure she'll sign anything you want,' said Oli calmly, cutting across her, 'at the *signing!*'

He really needed to get Kendra to calm down before Ruby turned up. Otherwise, Ruby might take one look at the girl and run for the hills. Something told him she wasn't exactly comfortable with her newfound celebrity status, and unfortunately for Ruby – Kendra was a super-fan and about as rabid as they came.

'Aw!' said Kendra, sticking her bottom lip out. 'But-'

'If you promise me you won't leap on her this evening,' said Oli, 'I'll make sure you get a quarter of an hour alone with her at the shop to talk about writing, and the book... and whatever. Deal?'

'Seriously?!' breathed Kendra, her eyes going wide.

'Seriously,' said Oli, though he was already

wondering how Ruby would feel about him playing fast and loose with promises of *her* time.

'Okay, deal,' said Kendra. 'Erm... can I ask one more thing?'

'Go for it,' said Oli, unable to hide his relief.

'What's with the basket? You look like Little Red Riding Hood!'

'It's a picnic,' said Oli. 'I was going to buy Ruby dinner – and I forgot the kitchen's closed at the moment.'

'Oh,' said Kendra, raising her eyebrows. 'You know, that's kinda romantic.'

'Seriously - stop!' said Oli, shaking his head frantically. 'It's just good manners – besides, it's not like there's anywhere else to go for a meal in town, is it?!'

'Okay, fair point,' said Kendra with a shrug. 'So... what'd you get?'

'Sausage rolls,' said Oli.

'Eww!' laughed Kendra. 'Okay, you're right... definitely not romantic!'

'Buzz off!' he laughed, wafting his hands at her in the hope that she might get the hint.

'Fine!' sighed Kendra. 'I'm going, I'm going! Have a great date-'

'Kendra!'

CHAPTER 13

RUBY

The smell of fish and chips was all-pervading as Ruby stepped out of her bedroom. The tang of hot vinegar had been teasing her and making her stomach growl for the last ten minutes… and she was starting to regret turning her mum down in favour of shlepping down the hill to the Dolphin and Anchor.

Ah well, it was too late to change her mind now!

Ruby was freshly showered and – after obsessing about it for far longer than was necessary – she'd pulled on a pair of smart black jeans and a top she'd bought to wear at her Milan signing. She'd decided to go for a look that was pulled-together and business-like. Or… that's what she was aiming for. It had to be better than "dithery mess" – a look that would be far closer to the actual truth.

Above all - she didn't want Oli to think she'd dressed to impress *him.* Those days were long long

long gone. Long gone. And the more she repeated it to herself… the more she might actually believe it. Now all she had to do was escape the house without ending up stinking of hot vinegar and chip fat.

Pulling her bedroom door closed behind her, Ruby pelted down the stairs and made her way past her father's study, peeping inside as she went. The familiar sight of his greying head bent over a book while he absently nibbled on a chip brought a lump to her throat.

It was really no wonder that she had a thing for books - not when her dad practically lived in a cave full of the things, and preferred their company to actual people.

With a little sigh of regret that she couldn't join him in his blook-lined hermit hole, Ruby wandered through to the kitchen only to find her mum's version of exactly the same scene in progress. Her portion of fish and chips sat abandoned on the kitchen table, while she stood at the kitchen sink, scrubbing away at a pile of muddy objects with an ancient toothbrush.

'Find anything good?' said Ruby, stealing a chip and promptly regretting it. It was already lukewarm.

'Too soon to tell!' said her mum, peering closely at something that looked a bit like a torture device for dolls. 'But I'll win that trophy if it's the last thing I do.'

'I believe you!' chuckled Ruby. 'Right - I'm off to the Dolphin and Anchor.'

'Okay,' said her mum, not turning around.

'Mum?' said Ruby.

'Hmm?' said her mum, still scrubbing away.

Ruby paused. She wanted to ask if she looked alright. She wanted to ask if it was ridiculous to be nervous about meeting up with a boy she'd spent the happiest summer of her life with before breaking his heart. But... she couldn't. That sort of thing didn't come anywhere *near* Sally Hutchinson's comfort zone.

'It's nice to be back,' Ruby said quietly.

'That's good,' said her mum.

∼

Ruby let out a sigh of relief as she stepped out of the fishy-chippy-scented kitchen into the fresh air of the little back garden. Sure, it looked like it had a terrible case of chicken pox after her mum's enthusiastic hunt for a buried "odd object", but it was still quite pretty in the soft evening light.

That was the thing with Crumbleton - it was unfailingly pretty. It didn't matter which way you turned, the place was picture-postcard perfect. It was why the tourists loved it so much. Back when Ruby felt like she was stuck here, its sweetness had been enough to give her toothache. Now, though - after her long, self-imposed exile - it felt like a balm on her frazzled nerves.

Heading through the narrow passageway and onto the high street, Ruby turned her steps downhill. The

Dolphin and Anchor sat right at the bottom, just along from the City Gates. It was the only place in town with a bit of land attached. What used to be an old grass tennis court out the back now made for a shrub-lined garden - a good spot to nurse a pint or two in fine weather.

The hotel's position was perfect for visitors from out of town who didn't want to face the hill, and there was even a little carpark – a very rare thing in Crumbleton. If you were local, however, facing the steep walk home after a few too many drinks could be... interesting. Then, the uneven steps and quaint cobbles quickly turned into something of an obstacle course!

Shop windows gleamed at Ruby as she wandered past. The awnings might have been wound up for the night, and the signs on the doors flipped to "closed' - but every single window display was perfectly lit.

Ruby paused for a moment to admire a display of bright lollypops that had been strung across the sweet shop window with clear fishing wire, making the tastiest and prettiest of candy curtains. As she peered through the glass, she could just about make out the same wooden shelving she remembered from childhood, holding jar after jar full of old-fashioned treats. If they'd still been open, she might have been tempted to nip in and ask for a bag of cola cubes. They were Oli's favourites. As for her, she'd never been able to say no to those foamy bananas... even though they'd always made him pull a face.

'Come on, Rubes,' she muttered, stepping back and doing her best to drag herself out of memory lane before she got lost down there. It was time to face the present instead – the one that was waiting for her in the bar of the Dolphin and Anchor.

On one hand, Ruby was hoping that Oli would keep things strictly business. It would be easier if they just stuck to the topic of her book signing. On the other hand, though... she had a feeling she'd be secretly heartbroken if that's all they ended up talking about.

'Oh, grow up!' she huffed.

The poor guy didn't deserve to be met with her long-held mess of emotions. No doubt - as far as Oli was concerned - she was just a girl he'd once flirted with to make studying a bit more bearable. A fling that had taken him by surprise during that sweet, in-betweeny summer – after school and before college - when it had felt like all bets were off and the world was at their feet.

To Oli, she was probably just a distant memory... and in reality, that's all he should be to her too. Instead, he felt like the start of a story she'd been forced to abandon. A tale she'd been aching to follow all the way to the final chapter... until the book had been slammed shut on her.

'Breathe!' she whispered, picking up her pace and focussing on the sound of her footsteps on the cobbles.

She was working herself up into a proper tizz… and she wasn't even at the bottom of the hill yet. She glanced at her watch and then put on a burst of speed before she was officially late. Poor Oli - the guy didn't know what he'd let himself in for, did he?!

When the broad white frontage of the Dolphin and Anchor appeared in front of her at last, Ruby paused, panting a little as she tried to get her breath back. Her legs were twitching from the unaccustomed exercise - she'd been back for less than a day and she could already feel the effects of Crumbleton's hill! It was no wonder Oli had become such a talented runner - living here was the best kind of training you could get!

As for her – she'd clearly spent far too much time sitting at her laptop. There had been plenty of dashing around recently though – but the problem with book events was that they inevitably involved cake somewhere along the line! Thank heavens this was the last event in her diary for a good long time. She needed some proper exercise before launching herself into the next book. If there *was* a next book.

Ruby shook her head – stopping the thought dead before it had the chance to drag her down into the doldrums. She should be *excited*! After all, her career had taken off in a way that most authors dreamed of.

Yeah – but you weren't expecting the dream to be more like a nightmare, were you?!

Urgh! When had her head become so full of things she didn't want to think about? It was like she had to tiptoe around inside her own brain, doing her best to avoid it all.

Sucking in a deep breath, Ruby shook her head in an attempt to clear it as she scanned the windows of the hotel. Her eyes flitted from one navy blue frame to the next, searching each golden square of light for Oli's face.

No sign. Well… there was nothing for it but to head inside and face the music.

A wave of warmth and chatter hit her in the face as Ruby pulled open the heavy door and walked into the bar. She paused, blinking as she waited for her eyes to grow accustomed to the dim, golden light.

Several people turned towards her from their perches at the bar, and Ruby smiled and nodded at the various familiar faces. They all returned her smile before turning back to sip their pints.

Ruby breathed a sigh of relief. She'd been so caught up with the fact that she was going to have to talk to Oli, she hadn't considered there was a possibility that she might have to make small talk with the rest of the town too. Lucky for her, it looked like the current crowd were more interested in working on their drinks.

Glancing around, Ruby spotted Oli sitting at a little table right underneath the dartboard. She headed straight for him before she could change her mind.

'You came!'

Oli was on his feet before she'd even reached him.

He smiled at her and she felt her treacherous knees give a little wobble. She'd love to blame it on the hill… but who was she kidding? This time, it was all down to the tall, dimpled man standing in front of her.

Ruby stared at him. She'd barely had the chance to take him in when she'd found him in the bookshop earlier – but now she let her eyes drink their fill.

Oli had changed… but only in the fact that he'd grown into his youthful good looks. He'd always been cute, but now… well… he was practically edible.

'Of course I came,' she said, her voice coming out in a croak as she dropped her eyes to the table. There was a jar of yellow roses sitting to one side, and right in the centre was a wicker basket. 'Erm… what…?' she started, gesturing at it.

'The kitchen's closed at the moment,' said Oli, fidgeting a bit. 'I asked Ken if he'd mind me bringing some food with me - and I did a bit of a snatch and grab from the bakery before they closed. I hope… I hope that's okay?'

Ruby just nodded, mainly because her vocal cords seemed to have gone on strike. She couldn't count the number of times the pair of them had dashed into the bakery just before closing time to hoover up the leftover sausage rolls, pasties and crumbly crusts of lemon drizzle cake. Then they'd retreat with their haul… to eat and study and… and…

It had been their thing.

'Thanks,' she muttered at last. 'Definitely okay.'

Ruby suddenly realised that they were both still standing - hovering next to their seats. Oli looked more than a little bit awkward.

'Shall we sit?' she added, sliding into her chair without waiting for him to answer.

'The... erm... the flowers are for you,' said Oli, following suit. 'I had them at the shop, but I didn't get the chance to give them to you earlier. I thought you might... you might like them.'

She nodded and swallowed a ball of nerves that had lodged in her throat.

'They always used to be your favourites,' he said. 'I didn't know if-'

'They're lovely,' she said, deciding to let him off the hook. 'Thank you.'

'You're welcome,' he said. 'So... I guess we need to talk...'

CHAPTER 14

RUBY

'Talk,' echoed Ruby. 'Right… talk.'

'But first…' he drew the basket towards him. 'Here's a plate for you… knife… fork… napkin…'

He handed each item to Ruby as he went, and she softened when she noticed that his hands were shaking ever so slightly. Perhaps he was as nervous about this whole thing as she was?! It seemed unlikely – Oli had always been pretty sure of himself. Not cocky – just comfortable in his own skin with a no-nonsense, straightforward attitude to life. It was something she'd always loved about him.

'Earth to Ruby!' said Oli.

Ruby glanced up to find him smiling at her, and she had to do her best not to melt.

'Sorry,' she said quickly. 'I was miles away!'

'Anywhere nice?' he laughed, handing over a slightly greasy paper bag.

Ruby just shrugged. She wasn't about to answer that. Instead, she opened up the bag and took a sniff.

Sausage rolls. YUM!

It looked like everything about this little meeting was going to act as a time machine. She reached in and gingerly extracted a golden pastry, placing it carefully on her plate before handing the bag back to Oli.

'Ta!' he said. 'There's ketchup in there for you too.'

Ruby grinned at him. She couldn't help it. The fact that he'd always kept a bottle of ketchup in his rucksack just for her had been a long-standing joke. It might also explain why she hadn't eaten ketchup in six years.

She really *was* a headcase!

'Thank you!' she said, reaching into the basket for the bottle.

'My pleasure,' he laughed. 'I wasn't about to face the wrath of Ruby by forgetting the red stuff. Made that mistake once… never again!'

The "once" in question had been one of their early study sessions. Oli had returned from the bakery with the usual haul… and a bottle of salad cream. She'd nearly called things off right there and then. It had taken a *lot* of making up. Not that either of them had minded that bit.

Ruby gave herself a mental kick and helped herself to a dollop of ketchup.

'So,' said Oli, taking a bite of his sausage roll. 'Like I said… we need to talk.'

Ruby nearly choked on her first mouthful.

'We do...?' she spluttered.

Oh hell, did they really? She had so many questions... but couldn't they just sit there in silence, eat their sausage rolls and pretend nothing bad had ever happened between them?

Couldn't they pretend she hadn't just spent the loneliest six years *not* living her life - because he hadn't been there with her.

'Drinks!' she said, shooting to her feet, jostling the table and setting the plates rattling. The bottle of ketchup fell over with a dull thud.

'Oh!' said Oli. 'Let me-'

'I insist!' said Ruby, her voice slightly too loud.

Oli looked suspiciously like he was trying to smother a smile.

'What do you fancy?' she added in a strangled voice.

'I'll take a pint of lager, please.'

Giving him a curt nod and doing her best to ignore the fact that his lips were twitching, Ruby darted towards the bar. She stood with her back to Oli and their little picnic, desperately trying to pull herself together. She was being ridiculous - and if she didn't calm down, it was just going to go from bad to worse.

This was a business meeting, for heavens' sake! All she had to do was talk to him calmly. Like an adult. She needed to stick to the plan – play it nice and safe, stay away from the past, and focus on the ins and outs of the event.

The problem with this most excellent plan was that she had so many questions... and now that he was right there across the table, they felt more important than talking about book stuff.

Ruby really wanted to know what he was doing back in Crumbleton... and why had he bought the bookshop, of all places? She shook her head. No. She just needed to get this job done - stay on topic - and then get the hell out!

'What can I get for you?'

Ruby glanced at the young girl who'd just appeared in front of her and was relieved to find it wasn't someone she knew. A touch of anonymity was exactly what she needed right now.

'A pint of lager and a ginger beer please,' she said, making a snap decision to stick to soft drinks. The last thing she needed was for her already slender grip on things to be loosened even further by alcohol.

'Wow,' said the girl, as she started to pull Oli's pint. 'I can't believe I'm serving *the* Ruby Hutchinson! I'm Kendra, by the way.'

Ruby's smiled awkwardly at the girl.

So much for anonymity!

'You're an awesome writer,' breathed Kendra. 'I love your book. It's just amazing. I can't wait for you to sign it for me!'

'Well, thanks,' said Ruby. 'So... you're coming to the event?'

'Yeah,' said Kendra, who looked like she was practically vibrating with excitement. 'And Oli said I get fifteen minutes alone with you afterwards to ask as many questions as I like – only if I don't bug you this evening… but I *have* to tell you… it's so cool you came home for your last stop on the tour. I'm well chuffed. I think I got the first ticket!'

'Erm… great,' said Ruby, wrapping her hands around the drinks. 'Good for you.' As usual, she had precisely zero idea about how she should respond. She never knew what to say when someone liked her writing. Of course, part of her was pleased – but she always found it a source of pure amazement that random strangers enjoyed her work. 'I'll… see you on Thursday, then.'

Ruby smiled awkwardly at Kendra and then hot-footed it straight back to the table.

'Here,' she said, plonking Oli's drink down in front of him.

'Meet your biggest fan?' he chuckled.

'You knew?' said Ruby, her eyes widening.

'What, that Kendra's obsessed with you and your book?' he said. 'Oh, I knew! She works for me every Saturday, but she's been into the shop practically every day since you agreed to the signing - just to double check her name's still on the list and that you haven't cancelled!'

'Wow,' said Ruby in a low voice. 'She's… a lot. I

mean, really lovely but... wow! And what's all this about promising her an exclusive interview?'

Oli rolled his eyes. 'Yeah, sorry about that, but it was the only way to buy you any peace this evening. I would have warned you - but you did your great escape thing before I got the chance.'

'Sorry,' muttered Ruby.

'No need to apologise,' said Oli with an easy shrug, taking a sip of his pint. 'The look on your face was priceless, though - best bit of entertainment I've had all day!'

'Oh hush,' muttered Ruby, reigning in the temptation to stick her tongue out at him like she'd done a million times before.

'You know, I've been wondering how the introverted little bookworm was dealing with all the fame,' he said, raising one eyebrow. 'And now I know.'

'You know nothing, Jon Snow,' she sighed.

'Is that right?' he said. 'Well... all I'll say is that I wasn't really expecting to recognise Ruby Hutchinson - celebrity author. Especially when I got that cut-out thingy they made me put in the window.'

Ruby wrinkled her nose.

'I do recognise you, though,' said Oli, watching her closely. 'You're still the Ruby I remember, and... it's a nice surprise.'

Ruby watched him from underneath her lashes as he took another sip of his drink... and realised she felt exactly the same. Sitting in front of her was the person she used to know better than anyone else in the entire world - the guy who'd turned out to be so much more than the meathead jock she'd assumed he'd be.

'Right then!' said Oli, clapping loudly, making her jump.

It did the job, though - the noise had broken the spell. Suddenly she was back in present-day Crumbleton, sitting across from a man she'd once spent a summer with. She was a visitor - not quite at home... but then, nowhere was home anymore.

'Right then,' she repeated quietly.

'Let's talk about your signing,' said Oli.

'Oh,' she said. 'Yeah. Okay.'

Ruby reached for her glass and took a sip of her ginger beer. It was the reason they were both sitting there, after all.

'Now, I've gone back through all the emails from Bobbi and Ben,' said Oli. 'I've got the brand of bottled water you asked for – still and sparkling, there are plenty of notecards too. I *did* have a bit of an issue getting holographic ones, but I managed to get metallic, and-'

'Wait – what?!' laughed Ruby in surprise. 'You're kidding me!'

'Erm... not kidding,' said Oli. 'I can forward the emails to you if you'd like?'

'God no – no thanks!' she said quickly. Heads were

going to roll when she got back to London! It was just the kind of thing she hated… and her team had *done* that? To Oli?!?! He must have thought she'd turned into a total diva. 'What else did they ask for?'

'Someone to be on hand to turn pages for you while you read, a bowl of fresh tomatoes – which I thought was seriously weird - oh, and a new toilet seat to be installed on the morning of the signing!' he said, raising his eyebrows.

'Okay – now you're making it up!' said Ruby, her eyes wide with horror.

'Okay,' laughed Oli, 'maybe I added that last one. But the others are true.'

'I'm going to kill them,' she sighed, shaking her head. The terrible two had clearly decided that some end-of-tour hijinks were in order. They'd obviously decided that it was safe to have a little joke at her expense because she knew the bookshop owner.

'Sorry, Ruby,' said Oli. 'I should have-'

'Don't *you* apologise,' huffed Ruby, picking up her sausage roll and dunking it into her puddle of ketchup. 'I should have called to confirm the details myself.'

'Erm… isn't that the whole point of having people on your team?' laughed Oli.

'Not for much longer!' said Ruby darkly – though she didn't really mean it… deep down. Very deep down right now.

'Don't look so horrified,' chuckled Oli. 'I always knew you were a diva deep down.'

'Am not!' she squeaked, completely indignant.

Oli snorted. 'Chill - it's fine - I'm just joking. You know – it's so good to have you back for a few weeks. I was chuffed when Bobbie mentioned you were staying in town for a while.'

'Yeah well, she got that bit wrong too.'

The words were out of Ruby's mouth before she could stop them.

'What?' said Oli. 'You're not serious?'

'I've got an open-ended ticket,' she said with a shrug, 'but I'm leaving straight after the event on Thursday.'

The smile dropped off Oli's face and he looked… hurt.

'Do you really hate this place so much?' he said quietly. 'I mean, what happened to make you stay away for so long? I thought you were happy here… you seemed happy when…'

He trailed off, shifting uncomfortably in his chair.

Ruby swallowed. 'I didn't mean… it's just… I…' It was her turn to trail off. Why was she getting so flustered here? She didn't have to explain herself. Yes, she'd left Crumbleton behind her, and Sure, she hadn't exactly built herself a life in London – but she'd certainly forged a career for herself instead. 'I don't hate Crumbleton. It just brings back a lot of memories.'

'But not good ones?' said Oli.

Ruby frowned at the look he was giving her. He didn't get to look hurt. Hadn't he left Crumbleton in his rear-view mirror too? Just because he was back now - it didn't mean she should feel guilty because she wasn't.

Of *course* there had been good times. Crumbleton hadn't been a bad place to grow up... but she'd felt so stuck those last few years, so hemmed in and trapped - until that last summer when the little town had come alive. Because of him. Then he left.

'Look,' she said, her voice tight. 'I'm sorry, but I'm really not up for a trip down memory lane right now.' She dropped the remains of her sausage roll onto her plate and brushed the crumbs from her fingers. 'I'm sorry. I'm exhausted. Let's just go over any details I need to know about the event.'

'Oh,' said Oli, 'okay - I understand. You've had quite a trip.'

Ruby shot him a tight smile.

'So, we'll start at ten and aim to be done by twelve-thirty. You can do the reading first, then a question and answer session with the audience - and then plenty of time for signing afterwards.'

'You want a reading?' she said.

'Erm... it's kind of the main draw to the event,' said Oli.

'Oh.' Ruby swallowed.

She'd had to do exactly the same thing at all the other venues... but for some reason, she'd blocked out the idea of having to do the reading here. After all, she was going to know most of the people in the audience. They weren't going to be the usual nameless, faceless crowd.

'Is that okay?' said Oli, looking concerned.

'Yes,' she said quickly. 'Of course.'

'Cool.'

Ruby wished her heart would calm down. She needed air. She needed space. She needed to get out of Crumbleton!

'You know I don't really need posh bottles of water, right?' she said, feeling like she'd been painted as a bit of a knob by her team.

'What about the chocolate-covered pretzels?' said Oli raising an eyebrow. 'Because I've bought in a hundredweight.'

'You… you have?' she gasped.

'Nah - not really,' said Oli, winking at her, 'but I can get some if you still like them?'

Ruby shook her head. Damn him and his ridiculously good memory.

'Okay… well that's it really,' he said. 'Nice and simple - hopefully we'll sell loads of books and have a blast. I'm really looking forward to it.'

'Right,' said Ruby, nodding on autopilot. 'Right, it'll be good. Well… I'll see you there then?' She got to her feet.

'You're leaving?' he said. 'Already?'

Ruby stared down at her half-eaten sausage roll, the

ginger beer she'd taken just a sip or two from... and made up her mind.

'Yeah. Sorry - I'm shattered.'

'Oh,' said Oli, looking crestfallen. 'Okay - I get it.'

Ruby threw on her jacket and smiled at him. 'Thanks, then.' She cleared her throat awkwardly. 'I'll... see you.'

Making a dash for the main door with her head down, Ruby felt inexplicable tears prickling behind her eyes. Why couldn't she just be a normal human being for once? Why couldn't she have relaxed, chatted and reminisced – and maybe asked him some of the questions that had been prodding her in the back of her brain all day? But no - here she was - doing a runner yet again.

Pushing her way out of the bar into the evening air, Ruby marched towards the City Gates, taking the cobbles at a reckless pace. She didn't slow down until she'd scooted under the archway – eventually coming to a halt a couple of steps outside of Crumbleton.

Taking a long, slow breath, she stared out across the surrounding marshland, willing her hot cheeks to cool down.

'Rubes?!'

Oli's voice made the hairs on the back of her neck tingle. There had been so many times over the years she'd dreamed about hearing his voice again.

Still - she really couldn't handle talking anymore

this evening. She was tired and over-emotional, and something told her she was a hair's breadth away from doing something ridiculous if she got too close to him before she'd had the chance to have a good, long sleep.

'Ruby?' This time his voice was soft - and right behind her.

Hoping she'd managed to arrange her features into a vaguely normal expression, Ruby turned to look at him.

'Yeah?' she said. There was no heat in her voice. She just sounded exhausted.

'You... you forgot these.' Oli held the jug of yellow roses out towards her.

Ruby paused for a long moment before reaching out and taking them. Their sweet scent drifted up to her and suddenly, the tears she'd felt prickling behind her eyes felt dangerously close to falling.

'Thanks,' she said quietly. 'They're lovely.'

'Rubes, will you...' Oli cleared his throat and Ruby raised her eyebrows. 'Actually, never mind.'

'Never mind what?' she said.

'Well... I was wondering... would you spend tomorrow with me?'

'What, in the shop?' said Ruby in surprise. 'I mean, I guess I could pop in and sign-'

'No,' said Oli. 'No, I mean... can we spend tomorrow... together.'

'Oh!' said Ruby.

This was a bad idea.

The worst.

She should definitely say no and get out of there asap.

'Okay then.'

CHAPTER 15

OLI

'What if she doesn't come?' said Oli, running his fingers through his hair for what had to be the thousandth time that morning - and it wasn't even nine o'clock yet.

'Dude, she'll come,' yawned Caroline, sinking into her office chair and rubbing her face. She looked like she'd quite fancy a nap on her desk. 'I cannot believe you talked me into traipsing all over Crumbleton before breakfast!'

'You owed me one,' said Oli.

'Erm… how exactly?' demanded Caroline.

'Because you're my cousin,' he said simply. 'Anyway… you're right… she'll come…'

After more than an hour of dashing around, making sure everything was ready for his grand plan, the pair of them had retreated to Caroline's office for a much-needed coffee. As tempting as it was, they couldn't risk heading into the café in case they bumped into Ruby. That would spoil everything.

'But... what if-' Oli started again.

'Oh my sainted granny pants!' huffed Caroline, glaring at him. 'If I'd known the pair of you being back in the same town was going to mean I'd end up losing sleep, I'd have talked Ruby out of coming myself!'

'To be fair, I don't think it would have taken much doing,' said Oli with a sigh.

He already knew for a fact that Ruby had done everything in her power to wriggle out of coming back to Crumbleton. Her publishing team had been surprisingly open about the fact that they were having a hard time getting her to agree to it... and that was when she'd thought she'd be dealing with Reuben! If she'd known the truth, there was no way she'd be in town right now – no matter how much pressure her publishers applied.

Still - here they were. Not only was Ruby miraculously in town – but she'd agreed to spend a whole day with him.

She's not going to show! You know she only said that to get rid of you last night.

'Caaaar?' he whined, fixing his cousin with a beseeching smile.

'What?' she muttered. 'Actually, scratch that. Whatever it is, the answer's "no."'

Oli stuck his bottom lip out until Caroline let out a long sigh. 'Fine - what?'

'Will you text her for me? Just to put me out of my misery?' he said.

'And say what?' she laughed. 'Oh I know - "I've just spent the last two hours helping my idiot cousin set up the most ridiculous date ever, so you'd better turn up. Oh – and you owe me sleep."'

'Erm - no - definitely not that,' said Oli. 'Urgh, I'm so nervous!'

Caroline stared at him for a long moment, then her face softened. 'You are the softest, daftest idiot in the world - you know that, right?'

He smiled and nodded miserably.

'Fine,' she sighed. 'I know what to say.'

'You do?'

She nodded. 'Sure fire way to check that she's at least *planning* on turning up.'

'How?' said Oli.

'I'll offer her an alternative,' said Caroline with a little shrug. 'I'll invite her to have lunch with me over at Crumbleton Sands. Good plan, right?'

'No! Terrible plan,' said Oli, shaking his head. 'What if she cancels on me to hang out with you?!'

'Hmm,' said Caroline. 'Well then, my old chum – that would definitely give you your answer. If that happens - you've got even bigger problems than you think!'

'That's really not reassuring!' said Oli, letting out a surprised laugh.

'You want me to send it or not?' said Caroline.

Oli blew out a breath and ran his fingers through his hair again.

'You seriously need to stop doing that,' she said, her fingers flying over her phone screen. 'You look like a porcupine.'

'Okay - send it!' he said, doing his best to flatten the spikes again. 'But if she does opt for lunch with you instead - I'm totally gate-crashing!'

Caroline snorted.

'Actually, wait!' said Oli. 'I've changed my mind!'

'Too late!' crowed Caroline. 'Already sent it.' She tossed her phone down onto her desk and shot him a triumphant grin. 'You know, you should be thanking me anyway. If it wasn't for me, you and Ruby would never have even crossed paths in the first place.'

'We totally would have!' huffed Oli. He knew he sounded like a sulky teenager, but he couldn't help it.

'Yeah right!' smirked Caroline. 'You were never off the sports field long enough to meet *any* girls… other than cheerleaders. There's no way you'd have discovered our favourite bookish waitress – especially considering she spent all of her spare time either in the bookshop or in front of that typewriter of hers!'

'Fine… you *might* have a point,' said Oli. 'But I'm not sure about thanking you. You're basically owning up to the fact that it's your fault I went to America with a broken heart and never got over it.'

'Yeah right,' muttered Caroline. 'I'm sure you were sad and all that, but I bet you got over it fast enough.'

Oli shook his head slowly. His cousin couldn't be more wrong... but did he really want to go there with her right now? Did he want the biggest gob in Crumbleton to know there hadn't been *anyone* in his life since Ruby?

'You're serious, aren't you?' said Caroline, watching him closely.

'Serious?' he hedged.

'About Ruby,' she said, looking like the truth was dawning on her by the second. 'You're still in love with her, aren't you?'

'Love?' spluttered Oli. 'I never said love.'

'You didn't need to!' said Caroline. 'Wow... and just for the record, it's not my fault.'

'You introduced us,' said Oli.

'Yeah, but I wasn't the one who sent you off to America and made sure all ties between the pair of you were cut!' said Caroline.

'That's true,' said Oli.

'I still can't believe he did that,' said Caroline.

Oli nodded slowly.

'I know it's mean to speak ill of the dead and all, but Uncle Mike could be such a prick sometimes!' said Caroline.

Oli let out a surprised snort of laughter. 'If he could hear you now, you'd be in so much trouble!'

'Wasn't I always?' said Caroline with a shrug.

'Fair point,' said Oli. 'You know – dad wasn't *that* bad. Just strict... he always did what was best for me.'

'He always did what he *thought* was best,' countered Caroline. 'It doesn't mean he got it right very often.'

'Yeah well… no point running through all the "what ifs" now,' said Oli. 'I've wasted enough time doing that, and all it does is give you a headache.'

'Fair enough,' said Caroline.

'Dad told me everything, you know,' he said. 'Before he died, I mean.'

'Everything?' said Caroline.

'That he was the one who told Ruby not to contact me,' said Oli with a sigh. 'He told her she'd be holding me back – ruining my life. And he basically told me I'd be doing the same to her. He admitted he was the reason she never got in touch or took my calls… that he was the one who split us up. He apologised.'

Oli paused and watched as Caroline chewed her lip – looking like she was half sorry for him and half ready to punch a wall.

'Well,' she huffed, 'at least he said *something*.'

'Yeah well – that's in the past,' said Oli. 'The only "what if" I'm interested in right now is whether Ruby's going to turn up today or do another runner on me.' Oli paused and gulped down the last few mouthfuls of his already-cold coffee.

'Well… I have to hand it to you,' chuckled Caroline, 'you've managed to time the whole thing for maximum implosion-factor if it all goes wrong!'

'What do you mean?' muttered Oli. He wasn't sure he wanted to hear the answer.

'Just imagine how awkward tomorrow's event will be if today's date crashes and burns!' said Caroline.

'Dude… at least try saying it without that twinkle in your eye!' said Oli.

'My bad,' she said with a grin, grabbing her phone as it vibrated against the desk.

'What?' said Oli, having to restrain himself from grabbing the thing right out of her hands. 'Is it her? What does she say?'

'Looks like our girl is as ridiculous as you, cuz,' said Caroline, her eyes flicking down the screen.

'She's coming?' said Oli, annoyed at how strained he sounded.

'Looks like it!' Caroline nodded.

Oli let out a huge sigh of relief, feeling equal measures terrified and excited. 'I think my head's going to explode.'

'You've only got yourself to blame!' said Caroline. 'You're the one who came up with this hair-brained plan!'

'You *do* think she'll like it, though?' he said, scrambling to his feet.

'Well…' said Caroline, 'I guess you'll find out, won't you!'

CHAPTER 16

RUBY

Ruby cracked her eyes open and, for a brief moment, wondered where on Earth she was. Half sitting up in bed, she stared around. Piles of notebooks, posters on the walls, and soft vintage bedding. Of course - she was home - back in Crumbleton under her parents' roof.

Heaving a huge sigh, she flopped back down into the pillows and sneezed as a puff of dust tickled her nose. Shuffling over onto her side, she came face-to-face with the jug of yellow roses on her bedside table. A small smile appeared on her face - even as something squirmy wriggled in her stomach. Suddenly, the previous evening came back to her.

Roses from Oli.

The drink with Oli.

Oh hell... she'd agreed to spend the day with him. What on earth had possessed her?!

Ruby didn't have to look too far for the answer to that question - she'd have said pretty much anything to wriggle out of that awkward moment outside the City Gates last night.

Ruby blew out a long breath. A whole day together... what would they do? After all, there wasn't that much in Crumbleton to keep you occupied... unless you were a pair of teenagers, of course. Back then, they'd somehow managed to while away entire weekends at a time – but she somehow doubted she'd end up snogging the day away on a picnic blanket in Crumbleton Clump!

Just the thought of it made Ruby shiver, and she turned and buried her face to hide the soppy smile that had just appeared out of nowhere. Even now, the thought of sneaking around with Oliver Evans – school sports hero - was thrilling. She still couldn't believe this little nerd had somehow managed to capture his attention.

Oli had always been popular. He'd been sports captain and part of every single team their school had - but where he'd really shown exceptional talent was on the running track. He'd won practically every race he entered - and ended up being national youth champion many times over. It didn't matter how well he did, though - his father had always pushed him to do more... be better... train, train, train!

'Idiot,' muttered Ruby, clambering out of bed. She knew she should feel bad that Mr Evans had passed away, but it was hard to feel any kind of sympathy for the man who'd guilt-tripped her into cutting Oli out of her life.

But... maybe you can fix it?

Ruby shook her head. It was a dangerous thought, and one she hadn't let herself go anywhere near for a very long time.

Grabbing her bag, Ruby threw it onto the bed and started to rummage through the small selection of clothes she'd brought with her. Yanking out her least shabby tee shirt and a soft green cardigan, she stared at them for a long moment before shrugging. They'd have to do - after all, Oli already knew what she looked like. He was more than aware that she was the polar opposite of fancy.

Besides, this wasn't *really* a date, was it? He might have bought her flowers, but she wasn't about to kid herself that he had any intentions towards her other than catching up properly. At least... she was pretty sure that's what his intentions were.

Last night's skinny jeans... converse... tee shirt... cardigan. It would have to do. She was saving her little black dress for her signing tomorrow. Just the thought of the event made Ruby shudder, and she quickly put it out of her mind. If she wasn't careful, she'd just spend the entire day tied up in a big knot of nerves about it otherwise.

Clutching the threadbare towel her mum had handed her the previous night, Ruby headed out of her bedroom, praying the bathroom would be free. Perhaps the wrath of her parents' temperamental over-bath shower might knock some sense into her.

She'd just locked the door, propped her mobile against the tiles at the back of the sink, and was busy clambering out of her tartan pyjamas when the phone buzzed.

Hey you - how do you fancy meeting me for lunch today? I'll drive us down to the restaurant at Crumbleton Sands! Let me know? C x

Ruby stared at it for a long moment. There it was - the ready-made excuse she'd been praying for. It was the perfect reason to blow off this date with Oli. A huge part of her really wanted to say yes. She'd missed spending time with Caroline, and lunch with her would be fun, easy, and long overdue. But... being back in Crumbleton wasn't about being fun and easy, was it?

Ruby chewed her lip for a long moment, staring at the screen... and then decided that perhaps she'd better be honest with herself for what felt like the first time in a very long time.

As nervous as she was about today, a part of her knew she needed to talk to Oli. She'd been frozen in time for far too long. She needed closure... and if that's all she got out of today, then it would be worth it.

Taking a deep breath, Ruby replied to the message with shaking fingers.

Can't, sorry. Long overdue conversations to be had with you know exactly who. See you at the signing tomorrow. R x

∼

Oli had asked her to meet him at the café – and in classic Ruby style, she was ten minutes early. Crossing the cobbles, she stopped briefly in front of the window and peered inside. There wasn't any sign of him yet. If she wanted to back out, now was her last chance!

Much to Ruby's surprise, she realised that the uneasy sensation in her stomach wasn't nerves or fear anymore… it was excitement. She wouldn't be backing out now.

Grabbing her mobile from her back pocket, she glanced at the screen. Nothing.

'Huh,' she muttered. She'd expected some kind of response from Caroline - even if it was just a thorough ribbing – but she hadn't heard a squeak. Shrugging, she thrust the phone back into her pocket. No doubt her friend would demand a thorough de-brief after her day with Oli. As long as she didn't ask for it right in the middle of the signing tomorrow, Ruby was up for it.

'Morning Ruby!'

Ruby jumped and looked around. 'Mrs Prescott!'

The once-familiar face of her favourite primary school teacher was beaming at her. 'I cannot wait to hear you talk about your book tomorrow.'

'You're coming?' said Ruby, as the familiar

awkwardness started to creep over her.

'I wouldn't miss it, Ruby,' she said, her smile growing even wider. 'I always knew you'd do something special. I have to say, I'm incredibly proud of you.'

'Thanks,' mumbled Ruby, shaking her head by force of habit. 'It's nothing really…'

'Don't do that,' said Mrs Prescott gently, shaking her head. 'Don't make something so magnificent smaller than it deserves to be. You've achieved something remarkable - and I'm excited to see what's next!'

'I…' she paused and just nodded instead. 'Thank you.'

She felt like she'd just been told off at the same time as receiving the hugest compliment. It was all quite a lot to take, considering it wasn't even nine o'clock in the morning yet!

'I'll see you tomorrow,' said Mrs Prescott, patting her arm before continuing on her way up the hill.

Ruby stared after her for a long moment, feeling like something had just shifted deep inside her.

'Don't be an idiot!' she muttered, before turning and pushing her way inside the café.

'You're not on the rota for today!' laughed Mabel the moment she spotted her. 'Can't stay away, can you?'

'Not if there's a cup of coffee and a pastry in the offing,' said Ruby. Oli might not be there yet, but that didn't mean she couldn't make a start on proceedings!

'Are you happy to serve yourself while I get Stuart's breakfast bap ready for him?' she said, nodding over to Stuart Bendall, who was sitting at his usual table right at the back of the café. The owner of the hardware and general goods store had been coming in for his breakfast bap like clockwork ever since Ruby's first day on the job - and there was no way she was going to get in the way of his routine now!

'You carry on,' laughed Ruby. 'Oli will be here in a minute - I'll make ours.'

'He's not coming,' said Mabel cheerfully.

'Wait… what?' said Ruby, feeling like she'd just swallowed a concrete block as heavy disappointment dropped into her stomach.

'He was here really early,' said Mabel with a shrug. 'Asked me to tell you that he wouldn't be here to meet you. He left you this.'

Mabel handed her a piece of folded printer paper with her name scrawled across it.

'Erm… thanks,' said Ruby.

'You get yourself that coffee,' said Mabel, smiling at her kindly. 'I'll be out the minute I've got Stuart's bap done and you can tell me all about it.'

'All about what?' said Ruby.

'All about that look on your face,' said Mabel, raising an eyebrow.

'What look?' muttered Ruby.

'The one that says someone's just cancelled Christmas,'

CHAPTER 17

RUBY

Ruby watched as Mabel retreated to the kitchen. Then she stared aimlessly around the café for a moment before glancing down at the folded note in her hand.

'Coffee first,' she sighed, tucking the note into her jeans pocket along with her disappointment. She was desperate to see what it said, but she wanted to find a discreet corner to hide in before she opened it.

She felt... crushed. That was the only word for it. As much as she'd been nervous about spending the day with Oli, she now realised how much she'd been looking forward to it too.

Loading up her puck with enough coffee grounds to keep an entire town buzzing for hours, Ruby set about making herself an elaborate, triple-shot latte complete with hazelnut syrup. Her heart hurt... and only an extra-ginormous dose of caffeine and sugar could have a hope of covering it up.

As soon as she was done giving the coffee machine a careful clean, Ruby carried her drink towards the back of the café. She chose a table right in the corner and tucked herself into a chair with her back to the rest of the room. No matter what the note said, at least she'd be able to react to it without everyone else reading every word of it reflected on her face!

After savouring several slow, sweet sips of her coffee, Ruby put the cup down and yanked the note back out of her pocket.

Ruby,

Everything looks better with coffee inside you! Ask Mabel for one of those ones full of syrup that you love. Do you remember those? The ones that always threatened to blow your head off with every sip and kept you talking at nineteen to the dozen. Oh, those study sessions were fun! Me - ready to drop off to sleep, and you - quizzing me until gone midnight. Eat a pastry too - gotta keep your strength up! For the record, I'm really sorry I'm not there to meet you - promise this'll be way more fun though!
I'd love to play a game if you're up for it?

Ruby paused and glanced over her shoulder just to double-check check she was still on her own and that Mabel hadn't decided to sneak up to take a peek over her shoulder. The only person anywhere nearby was Stuart, and he was busy tapping away at his phone. She quickly turned her attention back to the paper in her hand.

Remember you once told me that you used to like doing treasure hunts around the town?

'What?' she laughed in surprise. How on earth had he remembered? She'd once told him how her mum had been too busy to take her out on her birthday. Instead, she'd sent Ruby on a treasure hunt around all the different shops in town. Every clue she solved had told her what she should buy, and where she should go next.

It should have been the loneliest birthday ever - but Ruby had loved every second of it. She'd slowly filled her "birthday adventure basket" with all manner of goodies, and the whole thing had ended in a glorious birthday tea party with her parents when she got home.

Ruby swallowed. Oli might have remembered… but she'd almost forgotten the precious memory. She felt a sudden rush of love for her mum and dad. They might be *different*… but maybe they'd always known her better than she'd ever really given them credit for.

Taking a deep breath, followed by a fortifying sip of super-coffee, Ruby carried on reading.

Since you're only back for a few days - it's time for a treasure hunt! To start with... you need your adventure basket. Maybe if you turn around right now, you'll find it waiting for you. Yes?
Solve the clues. Have fun, whatever you do!
Oli
Ps remember what our English teacher always told us - beginnings are important.

Ruby frowned, re-read the bewildering PS a few more times and then - feeling like a bit of an idiot - turned around.

'Hey Ruby!'

Stuart was looking right back at her, holding up a beautiful wicker basket - the type they sold down at Bendall's.

'Hi!' she said. 'Is… erm… is that for me?'

'Yep!' he said cheerfully. 'Special delivery.'

'Oh wow,' she laughed. 'Thank you!'

Stuart shrugged good-naturedly. He'd always been a man of very few words, but from what Ruby could remember of him, he had the kindest heart and treated his members of staff like family.

'You have a wonderful day now, Ruby,' he said, giving her a fond smile. 'And I'm very much looking forward to tomorrow.'

'You are?' said Ruby.

'We're closing the shop especially,' said Stuart, his face serious. 'It's a special occasion, that's for sure.'

Ruby smiled at him as a strange warmth bloomed somewhere in her chest. 'Thank you, I'm looking forward to it too,' she said, surprised to notice that she actually meant it. 'I'll see you there!'

Stuart gave her a little nod and then his face broke into a broad smile as he glanced over her shoulder. Ruby turned, only to find Mabel making her way towards them with Stuart's breakfast.

'My favourite part of the day!' he said, rubbing his hands together.

Ruby grinned and left him to devour what was basically an entire English Breakfast crammed between the two halves of a soft, white bun.

'Right, young lady,' said Mabel, joining her back at her corner table two seconds later and slipping into the chair opposite. 'What's up?'

It was a question Mabel had asked Ruby dozens of times over the years. The café had been Ruby's safe space, and Mabel had seen her through many teenage ups and downs.

Smiling at her old friend, Ruby reached across the table and took her hand. 'Absolutely nothing,' she said, giving it a squeeze.

'That's not what your face was telling me ten minutes ago!' said Mabel, peering at her suspiciously. 'If that boy's managed to upset you, I'll be having words! You've been back all of two minutes and-'

'It's fine,' laughed Ruby. 'I promise!' she added when she saw that Mabel was still in full-on protective mode. 'Look - here's the note he left for me.'

Mabel took it and flipped the paper open curiously. 'Goodness!' she chuckled as her eyes skimmed the note. 'This is all rather romantic, don't you think?'

Ruby shook her head automatically, causing Mabel to raise an eyebrow.

'Okay… maybe… you think?' said Ruby, wincing slightly at the note of hope that just snuck into her voice.

'Well… there's only really one way to find out,' said Mabel.

'What's that?' said Ruby.

'You're going to have to follow the clues and see where they take you, aren't you?' said Mabel, her eyes shining.

'There's just one problem with that,' said Ruby. 'I seem to be missing the next clue!'

'Maybe it's in the basket?' said Mabel, tipping it towards her for a good look inside.

'Anything?' said Ruby, who was already pretty sure there wasn't.

Mabel shook her head.

'Maybe he forgot,' said Ruby.

'No chance,' laughed Mabel. 'Anyone that goes to all this trouble isn't going to fall at the first hurdle. It must be in the note.'

'You think?' said Ruby, glancing at the words again.

'What did that PS mean?' said Mabel. 'The bit about your old teacher.'

"Ps remember what our English teacher always told us - beginnings are important," said Ruby, reading it again. She shifted uncomfortably in her chair.

'Why do you suddenly look like you're sitting on a hedgehog?' said Mabel in surprise.

'Well... me and Oli...' she paused. 'I just figured it was his roundabout way of reminding me that we had a bit of a *thing* when we were younger.'

Not that she needed reminding!

'Huh,' said Mabel, looking entirely unsurprised by the revelation of Ruby's biggest secret. 'Well... that explains a lot.'

'It does?' said Ruby.

'Well yes - he did suddenly start turning up in here towards closing time whenever you were around... and he always looked a bit like a love-sick moose!' laughed Mabel.

Ruby snorted, storing up the term "love-sick-moose" in case she ever got the chance to share it with Oli.

'Okay,' said Ruby, wiping tears of laughter from her eyes, 'but I'm not sure that gets us any further with the clue.'

'What exactly was your old teacher talking about?' said Mabel. '*Beginnings are important.* Beginnings of what - stories?'

'No - she was a total grammar freak,' said Ruby. 'She

was always going on about sentence structure and… ohhhh'

She quickly scanned the note again.

'Ohhhh *what?!'* said Mabel.

'Can I borrow your pen?' said Ruby, excitement wriggling in her stomach.

Mabel handed her the order pen she kept tucked behind her ear, and Ruby started to circle the first letter of each sentence.

READ TO ME
FIRST MY SHOP

'Wow - that note took some writing!' said Mabel, her eyes wide with amazement. 'What does he mean - "read to me"?'

'When I helped him to study for his exams, we used to read the set text to each other,' said Ruby.

'What was the text?' said Mabel.

'Persuasion,' said Ruby.

'Well then,' said Mabel, 'looks like you'd better go find him at the bookshop!'

'If he's there, it'll be the shortest treasure hunt known to mankin,' laughed Ruby, downing her coffee before getting to her feet and grabbing the basket.

'If he's not there, my advice would be to check inside all the copies of Persuasion he's got in stock!' said Mabel.

COMING HOME TO CRUMBLETON

With her new basket dangling from the crook of her arm, Ruby pushed her way into the bookshop. The familiar tinkle of the bell above the door seemed to echo somewhere in her chest. She was giddily happy... all because of Oli and his ridiculous game.

'Ruby!'

The excited squeak from behind the desk definitely didn't come from Oli.

'Oh, hi... Kendra, right?' said Ruby.

'You remembered!' said Kendra, nodding gleefully.

'Is... is Oli here?' she said.

Kendra shook her head. 'Nope - but I'm not going to tell you where he is, so don't even ask!'

'Okay!' said Ruby. A tiny bit of disappointment that he wasn't there was battling with a huge dose of excitement that the game wasn't over yet.

This treasure hunt had only just started!

'He did mention you'd be coming in, though,' said Kendra, 'and he asked me to give you this. He said you'd know which book to look at.'

Ruby reached out and took the small, ornate key from Kendra. It was the same one she'd tossed on the desk before running out of the shop the previous day. Now, it had a brown luggage label attached to it with a piece of string.

'Thanks,' she said.

Right there, in Oli's loopy scrawl were the words

check out chapter 6!

'The key's for-' Kendra started.

'The collectable books cabinet!' said Ruby, hurrying through the shelves towards the back. She'd bet anything Oli was talking about that beautiful, early copy of Persuasion she'd been ogling the previous day.

'Oh!' she said, unable to mask her disappointment when she peered through the glass. It wasn't there.

'You okay?' said Kendra, coming to stand next to her.

'Yeah,' said Ruby, feeling daft. 'I just thought… erm, there was a book I spotted in here yesterday. I had my eye on it - I was going to buy it before I head home… but… I guess it's sold?'

'Which one was it?' she said

'Persuasion,' said Ruby. 'A gorgeous old copy - green and gold bindings?'

'Oh,' said Kendra, looking shifty. 'I'm really sorry… that one was reserved.'

'Gutted,' sighed Ruby. 'But if that's the case, I'm not sure what I'm looking for.'

Kendra frowned and scanned the little cabinet. 'I'm going to bet it's the one that stands out like a sore thumb!' she said after a couple of seconds, pointing at a scruffy little book that looked like it was falling apart at the seams. The spine was so cracked, it was impossible to read the title… but that didn't matter. Ruby knew exactly what it was.

Slotting the key into the lock, she opened the door

and gently took hold of it.

'It's another copy of Persuasion!' said Kendra in surprise. 'I'm no expert - but it doesn't *look* like a first edition or anything!'

'That's because it's not,' said Ruby. She flipped open the cover and pointed at a name scrawled inside in biro.

Oliver Evans. Class 12A.

'Oli's old school copy?' said Kendra.

'Yep!' said Ruby, flicking through the familiar pages.

'Wow – look at the state of it,' said Kendra, staring at the pages as they fluttered past, littered with pencil lines and copious biro notes crammed into the margins. 'I thought annotating was a new thing!'

'Nah… and it was the best way to get things to sink into his skull,' said Ruby, running a finger over the heavy lettering. This poor book hadn't stood a chance with Oli around! 'He had to pay to replace it once he was done, though - the school didn't want it back.'

'Erm… I can see why!' said Kendra. 'Still don't get why it's in here, though.'

'Chapter 6,' said Ruby. 'Let's see…' She turned the pages more slowly, searching for a clue. 'Okay - that's not subtle!' she laughed as a stark stripe of bright pink highlighter glowed at her.

'What's he highlighted?' said Kendra.

Ruby glanced at her. The young girl's eyes were wide, and she was clearly as invested in this little mystery as she was.

'Erm...' said Ruby, her eyes scanning the familiar words. 'It's a passage about having to look after naughty kids. *"But you know it is very bad to have children with one that one is obligated to be checking every moment; "don't do this," and "don't do that," or that one can only keep in tolerable order by more cake than is good for them."*'

The words "more cake than is good for them" had been underlined three times. Ruby grinned.

'I don't get it?' said Kendra, cocking her head.

'I think it's your boss's less-than-subtle hint that the next clue is in the bakery.'

'Where you can buy more cake than is good for you,' said Kendra.

'I reckon!' laughed Ruby. 'And... going by his first clue, I'd better take the book with me... if that's okay?'

'Fine by me,' said Kendra with a shrug.

'Thanks for your help,' said Ruby. 'See you tomorrow - I'm looking forward to your questions.'

Kendra's eyes went wide with excitement. 'Be ready to fill me in on what happens next today!'

∽

Over an hour later, Ruby found herself wandering into the bar of the Dolphin and Anchor. Her basket was full to the brim. A huge bag of goodies from the bakery had been joined by a bunch of flowers from the florist at the top of the hill, several bags of sweets from the sweet shop, and a set of colourful plastic cups and plates from Bendall's.

The last clue had told her she should head to the spot where the "captain hits his bullseyes."

'Ah hah!' she said, peering across the room at the dartboard in the corner. Sure enough, there was a dart lodged right at its centre with yet another luggage label dangling from it.

"Bring your own bottle," she read. Well, that was simple enough, given that there was a little arrow pointing straight down at a bottle of prosecco and two bottles of ginger beer sitting on the table below the dartboard. She flipped the label over hoping for more. Sure enough...

"It's time for a ride in the highest-ranking Captain's ship!"

"Rank" was underlined several times, and Ruby giggled, rolling her eyes. The first clue back in the café might have been a tough nut to crack, but they'd become easier and easier as she'd missioned her way around town.

Popping the bottles into her basket, Ruby dashed back outside and headed straight for the Dolphin and Anchor's little carpark at the back where Brian Singer - *captain* of the darts team - had his unofficial taxi *rank*. Sure enough, the gallant captain was sitting behind the wheel with a book propped open in front of him.

'Ruby - you found me!' he laughed as she tapped on the window to get his attention.

'How long have you been waiting for me?' she said, eyes wide - feeling like she should apologise for taking so long.

'No clue,' he said with an easy shrug. 'You know what it's like when you get lost in a good book!'

Ruby nodded and then froze. 'Oh… it's mine!'

'Loving it so far,' said Brian, grinning at her. 'Amazing writing!'

'Thank you,' said Ruby with a shy smile. 'I'm so glad you're enjoying it.'

Then she paused, pulling herself up. Where was the usual discomfort? Where was the need to shudder and shiver and escape? It was gone, and in its place was a quiet kind of pleasure that someone she knew and liked was getting enjoyment from something she'd created.

'Ruby?' said Brian, watching her with interest from the window.

'Oh - right, sorry!' she laughed, shaking her head. 'Do you have a clue for me - as the *highest-ranking captain* of Crumbleton?'

'Nope, no clue,' said Brian.

'Oh,' said Ruby, deflating. 'You sure?'

'Positive,' said Brian, popping a bookmark carefully between the pages of the book and stashing it in the glove compartment. 'But I am here to give you a lift!'

'Where to?' said Ruby, her excitement bubbling right back up.

'That's for me to know and you to find out,' said

Brian. 'Hop in!'

Ruby let herself into the back seat and popped the heavy basket next to her. She was half expecting this to be a huge joke - for Brian to turn straight back up the steep high street and simply drop her off somewhere near the top. Instead, he turned out of Crumbleton, passing through the City Gates and joining the winding road that led across the salt marshes.

'Let me guess... Crumbleton Sands?' said Ruby, leaning forward to interrogate him.

'Not very patient, are you?' chuckled Brian.

'Nope!' said Ruby. 'Okay, what about-'

'I'm not telling you!' said Brian in amusement.

'Well... definitely not the beach,' said Ruby, as Brian indicated and took a turn that led in the opposite direction. They rounded the base of Crumbleton hill and drove past the little wharf where the Marsh Ranger kept his boat. The road followed a winding path through the ever-changing landscape of the watery marshland, between the reedbeds, pools and rivers.

Ruby knew this route well. She'd taken it enough times as a kid on her bike. Ahead of them, as if in answer to her question, she spotted a little hill rising from the wetlands - a much smaller echo of Crumbleton. This one was covered in trees.

'Crumbleton Clump!' she said.

'Maybe,' hedged Brian, rather spoiling the mystery by coming to a halt at the tree line a few minutes later.

CHAPTER 18

OLI

This was the worst idea he'd ever had in his life!

Oli paced from one tree to the next, cursing himself for coming up with such an idiotic date… especially considering Ruby was such an epic flight risk.

It had all seemed like such a great idea when he'd roped Caroline in to help him set it up. Even when the pair of them had been busy running around town that morning - dashing into the various shops, calling in favours and leaving behind clues - he'd been convinced that Ruby would love it. He'd been so certain nothing could possibly go wrong.

Now, with far too much time on his hands to overthink it all, Oli had realised that there were a few fatal flaws in his genius plan. For one thing, he'd be repaying the various favours he'd called in for years to come. On top of that, by asking so many people for their help, he'd basically broadcast the fact that Ruby meant far more to him than a simple blast from the past. He wasn't going to live it down in a month of Mondays!

Still... it'd be worth it if Ruby had fun... *if* she turned up, of course!

'Shut up, brain!' he huffed, letting out a little laugh.

This was the other side of his grand plan he hadn't quite thought through properly. He'd been here for what felt like hours already. He'd given himself far too much time to set up, and now all he had left to do was tie himself up in knots while he waited.

As soon as the pair of them had finished their coffee, Caroline had given him a lift and dropped him off at Crumbleton Clump. In his head, Oli had figured that it would take at least an hour to set everything up and make sure it was perfect and ready for Ruby's arrival.

Not so much, though. It had taken just five minutes to string the woodland clearing with fairy lights, and another ten to line the path from the road to the clearing with dozens of tealights set in jam jars. Then he'd spread the tartan blanket out on a comfortable spot – and everything was ready in less than half an hour.

All he had left to do was wait for her... and pace.

And sit.

And obsess.

And pace some more.

Oli made another circuit of the clearing, checking everything for the umpteenth time.

'Yep. Still perfect,' he sighed. There wasn't a light out of place.

Wait... was that candle out?

'Get a grip!' he laughed, as the little flame fluttered back to life.

With a long sigh, Oli flopped down onto the blanket and made himself a promise that he wouldn't budge again until Ruby turned up... or it got so late he'd know for sure that she wasn't going to come.

Pulling his legs to his chest, he wrapped his arms around them and stared intently at the entrance to the candle-lined path.

'One, Mississippi... two Mississippies,' he muttered. 'Three... pfft!'

He promptly gave up and lay back on the blanket to stare up at the green canopy of leaves swaying far above his strings of fairy lights.

'She's going to come. She's going to come!'

He let out a huge yawn and his eyes fluttered closed. A gentle breeze brought the scent of the woodland to him - rich and earthy - and the sound of the rustling trees started to calm his taught nerves.

'She's going to come,' he yawned again.

CHAPTER 19

RUBY

Popping another foam banana in her mouth, Ruby leaned back on her elbows and stared at Oli. He was still fast asleep. She smirked. She'd arrived a good twenty minutes ago, having practically trotted up the tree-lined path, admiring the flickering candles in their glass jars as she went.

Then, she'd stepped into the magical clearing, with its canopy of fairy lights and huge red tartan picnic blanket – and nearly had a heart attack. The last thing she'd been expecting was to find Oli, spark-out on his back. Her initial blast of fear that there was something horribly wrong had been quickly put to rest by a soft snore drifting on the breeze.

'Sleeping beauty!' she chuckled, picking up her pink plastic cup and taking a sip of the ginger beer she'd helped herself to. She had a feeling Oli wouldn't mind that she'd tucked into some of the goodies from the basket while she waited for him to wake up.

Oli's ancient copy of Persuasion sat next to her on the blanket. Ruby had fully intended to dive into its pages and enjoy the pure nostalgia of the words. As it turned out though, watching him snooze peacefully in front of her proved to be far too alluring, and she'd quickly set the book down to gaze at the way the dappled light played across his face.

Suddenly, Oli let out a huge yawn and started to stir. Ruby watched with amusement as his face went from pure, relaxed peace - to confusion - to panic in just a matter of seconds. He scrambled up and then spotted her sitting just a few feet away.

'You're here!' he said in pained surprise.

Ruby grinned at him and raised her cup in a mock toast.

'Wait…' he said, rubbing his face, 'you've been here for… how long?'

'One and a half glasses of ginger beer and most of my foam bananas!' she chuckled. 'I did think about opening the bubbly, but that seemed a bit mean… I didn't want the pop to wake you up!'

'I'm *so* sorry,' he said, rubbing his face. 'I can't believe I fell asleep. I wanted this to be-'

'Shh!' said Ruby, shuffling closer to him. Reaching out, she placed a gentle hand on his knee. 'It's perfect.'

'But I-'

'I love it,' said Ruby firmly, catching his eye and holding it. 'I had so much fun with the clues.'

'Really?' said Oli, his face starting to relax.

Ruby smiled at him and nodded, feeling a strange sense of pride that she had the power to wipe away his frown lines and replace them with a tentative smile.

'The first one was a toughie... but after that, I got into the swing of it,' she said, unable to keep the amusement out of her voice. 'You know, it was a seriously sneaky way to get me to do all the hard work - shopping for our date while you snuck off for a nap!'

'I didn't mean to fall asleep - I was so nervous I barely slept last night,' said Oli, suddenly looking like an eighteen-year-old again. 'I got here way too early to set up... and then all I had left to do was wait and wonder if you'd come.'

'Of course I came,' said Ruby.

As she said the words, she suddenly realised how true they were. Wherever Oliver Evans was – she wanted to be there too. The only way she'd managed to ignore the constant magnetic pull of him all these years was to build an impenetrable defence between her present and her past. Now, parts of that protective wall had started to crumble and the forces were at work on her once more - as gentle as the tide and subtle as lightning.

The pair of them were... inevitable.

With the realisation came another dose of awkwardness, and Ruby suddenly realised she still had her hand resting on Oli's leg. She quickly pulled away and reached for the basket.

'I think I got everything!' she said brightly.

'Did Kendra crack and tell you everything?' said Oli with a small smile. 'She was so excited that you were going in this morning!'

Ruby smiled more easily again. 'Nah, she was brilliant… though I think our private Q and A tomorrow might just be her grilling me about today and extracting as many juicy details as she can get!'

'Just tell her you don't kiss and tell!' chuckled Oli.

'Is there going to be kissing?' said Ruby lightly, drawing the paper bag of bakery goodies out of the basket and setting it between them without making eye contact.

'You tell me,' said Oli.

He suddenly sounded a bit out of breath, though it could just be a yawn trying to body-snatch him.

'I… um… well…' said Ruby.

Oli sniggered.

'Git!' she said, nudging his leg with her foot.

'Wuss!' he retorted.

'Am not,' said Ruby.

'Prove it!' said Oli.

'Fine. Maybe I will,' said Ruby. 'When you least expect it.'

'Something to look forward t-'

Ruby didn't even let him finish the sentence. She turned towards him, pressing her lips against his - a dare she'd just won rather than the kiss she'd been dreaming about for years and years.

'Ha ha!' she laughed, pulling back to crow at his surprise, only for him to reach up and gently cup her face in his hands.

'Ha ha,' he said slowly, his voice gravelly as he leaned in to kiss her properly.

This time, it wasn't a dare between two teenagers. This was six years of longing and hope and regret and desire. The remains of Ruby's defences dissolved, and she melted into Oli.

∽

'I still can't believe you're here,' said Oli.

His voice was low and lazy, and Ruby felt it as much as she heard it. She was snuggled against him, cosied into the crook of his arm with her head resting against his chest. The copy of Persuasion lay unopened on the blanket next to them, and it was so reminiscent of their teenaged study sessions that Ruby felt like she'd climbed into that time machine again. Only this time, it was different. No one could send Oli away from her, and she didn't have to leave him behind either... not if she chose not to.

'I'm here,' she said simply.

Oli tightened his arms around her, pulling her into a warm hug that cocooned her from the rest of the world.

'Rubes… I want to tell you something,' said Oli. '*Need* to tell you something, actually. About my dad.'

'Caroline told me he'd passed away,' said Ruby. 'I'm really sorry.'

'Thanks,' he muttered.

She felt him shift a little on the blanket and followed suit, turning so that she was lying on her side, her head propped up on one arm, facing him.

'Is that why you came back?' she said gently.

He shook his head.

'Did you get injured? Is that why you decided to stop competing?' she asked.

'Nope,' said Oli. 'No,' he said again with a heavy sigh. 'I just wanted to come home… I wanted to investigate some of the "what ifs" I was busy tormenting myself with.'

'Like… the bookshop?' said Ruby.

'Working with books was definitely one of them,' he said. 'I always wished I'd had the strength to stand up for myself and follow my heart. I spent years living for someone else… and I decided it was time to try out some stuff for myself instead. Then dad got sick and he was gone so fast and…'

He paused, a look of confusion crossing his face as though he didn't quite know how to continue.

'You must miss him,' said Ruby, her heart sinking. There was no way she was going to be able to tell him everything now - not with him grieving for his father like this.

'I *do* miss him,' he said. 'But at least I got to be with him at the end. I got to say goodbye.'

Ruby nodded.

'Rubes - that's what I wanted to tell you,' said Oli, pinning her with his eyes. 'Before he died, dad told me what he said to you before I went to America... he admitted he was the reason you disappeared from my life.'

'It doesn't matter now,' she said quickly, shaking her head.

Of course, it *had* mattered - more than anything - for a very long time. But now she was back here with Oli... now they were talking...

'He only did what he thought was best for you,' she said.

'That's true,' said Oli, nodding slowly. 'He told me he was trying to protect me - but he also said he was trying to do the same thing for you, too'

'I-' she started, not really knowing where she was planning to go with the sentence.

'Those things he said to you?' said Oli. 'He basically said the same thing to me, too. Not to ruin your life. Not to hold you back. He said you had so much talent... and it wasn't fair for me to ruin your future.'

Ruby stared at him, her mouth slightly open.

'He also asked me to apologise to you – for him - if I ever got the chance,' said Oli. 'So... sorry... for my dad.'

'It's forgiven,' said Ruby, shaking her head.

And forgotten, she added silently to herself.

The breeze set the leaves above them rustling and Ruby sat up, feeling like she was coming out of some kind of trance.

'How about a toast?' she said, grabbing the bottle of bubbly.

'Sure,' said Oli, retrieving a couple of brightly coloured plastic flutes.

Ruby popped the cork and poured, then set the bottle into the basket for safekeeping before taking her drink from Oli.

'To your dad,' she said. 'Mr Evans.'

'To dad,' said Oli. 'And I think he'd ask you to call him Mike at this point!'

'To Mike,' Ruby added with a soft smile, before tapping the edge of her plastic cup against his and taking a sip.

'And… to the rest of today, and your amazing event tomorrow!' said Oli.

'I'll cheers to that,' said Ruby as a little spark of excitement ignited somewhere in the pit of her stomach. 'By the way, what *are* the plans for the rest of the day?'

'Drink the rest of this bottle, eat our picnic, read to each other…' said Oli, wiggling his eyebrows.

Ruby snorted. Why did she get the feeling he wasn't really talking about reading?!

'Great,' she said, her voice slightly husky. 'And… after that?'

'Well, Caroline pointed out that I'm being a complete Ruby-hog, considering you're planning on leaving right after the signing tomorrow,' he said.

Ruby shifted uncomfortably. Why did her original plan suddenly feel like a lead weight in her stomach?

'Anyway - I thought I'd better rectify that,' he continued. 'So Caroline is going to swoop over and pick us up when we're done here, and we're all going over to Crumbleton Sands for early drinks and food.'

'We are?!' said Ruby, her eyes lighting up in excitement.

'Yep!' he grinned. 'And then we're going to come home and help your mum.'

Ruby blinked. 'Huh?'

'She needs a hand getting her Odd Object entries up to the museum,' said Oli.

'How do you know that?' said Ruby.

'She told me when she came in to pick up her tickets for tomorrow,' he said with an easy shrug.

'She's... she's got tickets?' said Ruby, feeling like the rug had just been pulled out from underneath her.

'Are you kidding me?' laughed Oli. 'She's had them reserved from the moment you confirmed you were up for it.'

'I... I wasn't sure if they'd come,' said Ruby quietly.

'They'd never miss this,' said Oli. 'I know you don't always feel it, but they adore you, Rubes. They are *so* proud.'

Ruby nodded, staring down at the blanket. She

wasn't entirely sure if the tears that had just started to prickle at the corners of her eyes were going to make a break for freedom or not.

'Heads up, though,' said Oli, reaching out and stroking one finger over the back of her hand, 'she did mention that she was going to come up with a couple of humdingers for the Q and A!'

Ruby snorted. That sounded more like the mother she knew and loved.

'So,' he said, leaning forward and placing a gentle kiss on her forehead, 'let's make the most of this before Caroline ruins the mood… because we both know she's awesome at that! More bubbly?'

Ruby grinned at him and held out her glass, then changed her mind.

'Kiss first, please!'

CHAPTER 20

RUBY

Ruby wasn't due to arrive at the bookshop for at least another hour... or two, even... but she couldn't bear hanging around in her parent's kitchen a moment longer. She was too amped up for that!

Instead, she'd made a mad, early-morning dash to the bakery and then begged Mabel for the largest takeaway cups of coffee she could manage. Her old friend had gently suggested that perhaps chamomile tea might be a better choice, considering Ruby was practically vibrating with nervous energy already.

Ruby had won, though, and now she was standing in front of the gorgeous green and gold frontage, staring through the windows of the bookshop. It wasn't open yet, but she could see Oli moving around inside, tidying piles of books, shifting the wooden ladders out of the way, and wafting a feather duster around.

She could stand there and watch him all day - he looked both at home and slightly out of place at the same time. It was impossible to miss the coiled power in his movements. Oli might have kicked sports out of bed in favour of a life with books, but all those years of training were still evident in the hard lines of his muscles - his arms taught beneath his rolled shirt sleeves.

Ruby shivered as memories of their date the previous day flooded back - all those warm, stolen kisses on the blanket had been everything she'd tried *not* to dream about for the past six years. She'd loved every second of their picnic in Crumbleton Clump - but the rest of the day had felt even more intimate, somehow - even if they hadn't been alone for one second after leaving the woodland.

The day had disappeared in a wonderful muddle of laughing with Caroline over food, walking her mum up to the museum and then - on the spur of the moment - dragging her father out of his book cave as they made their way back down the hill to join Brian Singer for a night of darts at the Dolphin and Anchor. It had felt like they were… family.

'Get a grip!' she laughed.

What on earth was she doing, standing on Crumbleton High Street, ogling Oli through the bookshop window and being a soppy idiot? For one thing - she really needed to stay calm ahead of today's event and *not* send her blood pressure skyrocketing. For another - their coffee was getting cold.

Ruby shifted the cardboard tray containing the two cups so that she could tap lightly on the window with one finger. Oli glanced over his shoulder and the moment he spotted her, a huge smile split his face. It was as much as Ruby could do not to dissolve into a puddle of mush on the spot

'You're keen!' he said as he unlocked the door and took the tray of coffee from her.

'Not really,' said Ruby, wrinkling her nose. Her stomach had been in nervous knots ever since she'd woken up, and there was no point pretending otherwise - but there was something about admitting it out loud that instantly made her feel better.

'It'll be grand,' said Oli, leading the way inside. 'Blimey - I'd have thought you'd be more than used to this kind of event by now.'

'The difference is, none of those people knew me,' she said, flopping down into the armchair as Oli dropped into the bentwood chair behind his desk. 'They had no idea that I worked summers in the local café, that I failed my German GSCE or that I spent my spare time tutoring the cutest guy in town.'

'Thanks!' said Oli, giving her a huge grin. 'But… why does any of that make a difference?'

'Because everywhere else, readers came to the event

because of the book,' she said. 'Today they're coming because of me.'

'That's pretty special, if you ask me,' said Oli with a shrug.

'And terrifying at the same time!' said Ruby, eyeballing the oh-so-familiar embossed titling on a stack of her books sitting on the table nearby. 'Anyway - I wanted to repay your lovely picnic yesterday with some breakfast… before the chaos starts.'

'You mean you couldn't sleep and had to get out of the house before you went mad?' said Oli, raising an eyebrow. 'I remember exactly what you were like before an exam, Ruby Hutchinson!'

'Okay fine,' pouted Ruby. 'You've got me. But you do make a very good distraction!'

Oli winked at her and held her eyes for a long moment. Ruby felt her cheeks grow warm. Somehow, she knew he was thinking about the kisses they'd shared on the blanket the day before… just like she was thinking about the way they'd held hands as they'd ambled down the high street, chattering to her parents. Ruby still couldn't quite wrap her head around the moment her mum had peered down at their interlaced fingers and breathed the words "at last". They'd sounded very much like a sigh of relief.

'So, about today…' said Ruby.

She paused. Was she really going to say this?

Yep. Yes she was. After all, she'd waited long enough.

'It'll all be fine,' said Oli slowly. 'As long as you don't plan on doing a runner!'

'That's just it,' said Ruby, shifting uncomfortably.

'You're not going to disappear on me... are you?!' he said, his eyes going wide.

'Quite the opposite, actually,' said Ruby, shaking her head. 'I was wondering... what would you say if I told you I didn't want to leave this afternoon... that I wanted to stay in Crumbleton a bit longer?'

'I'd say stay forever,' said Oli, giving her an easy shrug.

A dollop of pure happiness slid into Ruby's stomach.

'We'll see,' she said grinning at him before taking a sip of coffee.

'Can I ask you something?' said Oli.

'Anything!' she said.

'How come Bobbie and Ben didn't come here with you?' he said. 'I mean - I'm not complaining - those two are mildly terrifying. I'm just surprised they abandoned you on your last stop after travelling all over the world with you.'

'They wanted to come,' said Ruby, 'but I really didn't want to come back to Crumbleton *at all*.'

'Yeah, I know,' said Oli, 'don't remind me!'

'Sorry!' she chuckled. 'Anyway, it was the only way I said I'd agree to it - on my own or not at all.'

'But why?!' said Oli.

'Honestly?' said Ruby. 'Because I wanted to make

sure there would be no one around to stop me if I decided to make a break for it before the signing.'

'You're not serious?' said Oli.

'Deadly,' said Ruby. 'But I promise, I'm not going anywhere, so you can breathe!'

Oli let out a long, jokey sigh, but something told Ruby he wasn't quite done with the questions just yet… and she realised that she really didn't mind. She no longer had anything to hide. In fact, she was ready to share pretty much everything with this man.

'So… why'd you stay away for so long?' said Oli. 'I wanted to ask you yesterday, but I didn't want to…'

'Spook me?' said Ruby.

'Exactly!' laughed Oli. 'Though to be fair, if finding me snoring in the woods didn't do that, I should have known pretty much anything else would be okay!'

'Yeah, you have a point,' she laughed.

'Anyway,' said Oli, 'you didn't know I was back in Crumbleton, so I know you weren't just doing it to avoid me, so…?'

'I was avoiding the ghost of you,' she said softly. 'The ghost of us, really. I had the best times of my life here… and the worst. I didn't want to deal with a bunch of memories. Ultimately, I couldn't deal with facing what I'd lost.'

'I get that,' he said nodding. 'It was kind of the same-but-opposite for me. Best and worst memories of my life right here in Crumbleton… but I wanted to wrap the whole lot around me like a blanket. I wanted to remember.'

Ruby got to her feet and walked over to him. Without saying a word, she dropped into his lap and wrapped her arms around him, not caring that they were in full view of the windows.

~

'"She swallowed her tears. After all, this was just the beginning."'

Ruby closed her book and silence descended on the shop.

People were squeezed into the space, spilling from the chairs, leaning against tables and even perched on Oli's desk. Dozens of pairs of eyes stared back at her.

Ruby shifted her weight, from one foot to the other – uncomfortable in the deafening hush. Should she say something? Should she tell them that was it – she'd finished? Should she-

A roar rose from the crowd, and suddenly the shop was filled with clapping and cheering and calls for "More! More! Another chapter!"

Ruby stared around as a strange rush of emotions hit her in the chest. Gratitude, pride… and…

Her eyes went to her mum and dad in the front row. Both of them were clapping along with the rest, and they were staring at her with identical looks of wonder on their faces. Ruby smiled back at them even as she bit the inside of her lip to stop her face from crumpling. She was close to losing it, and her dad nearly pushed her right off the edge as he mouthed three words at her.

Proud of you

Ruby felt a bit like she was adrift in a sea she was only just learning to swim in. She stared around again, this time searching for something - or someone - to anchor her.

'Thank you, Ruby Hutchinson!'

Oli's voice boomed from behind her. He was addressing the crowd as much as her, and they instantly began to settle - the noise levels subsiding into friendly murmurings.

Ruby felt his brief touch on her back, and she breathed a sigh of relief. There he was – her anchor.

'Right… now's the bit you've all been waiting for,' said Oli, easily commanding the crowd. 'Are you ready to give our Rubes a good grilling?'

Ruby turned to glare at Oli and, much to the amusement of the crowd, she gave him a good dig in the ribs with her elbow. Hands shot up all over the place, but Oli pointed straight at her mum, who had a broad smile on her face.

Uh oh!

Well, perhaps it was best to get the scariest one out of the way first!

'Sally?' said Oli.

Ruby's mum beamed. 'I'd like to ask... do you base your characters on real people?'

Ruby blinked. It was a question she'd been asked at every single event she'd done so far, and so removed from the terrifying inquisition she'd been expecting, she was caught completely off guard.

It was an easy question, and one she had a stock answer for. But... what if she actually told the truth for a change?

'You know,' she said, smiling at her mum, 'I get asked that a lot. And in the past, I've always said "no" and then gone on about how - as an author - you pick up inspiration from everywhere. Which is kind of true... but...'

She paused and glanced back at Oli who was watching her with interest.

'But... the answer is yes,' she continued, turning back to the crowd. 'This book is a love letter to every single one of you... you're all in there somewhere. Your smiles, your kindness, your quirks. Not as one character in particular - but in the essence of all of them.'

She paused again and took a shaky breath.

'I've been away from home for a very long time - and I spent most of it with my head in this book. So I filled it with all the people I love - all of you. I filled it with family. I filled it with home - so that I didn't feel so very far away from you all.'

As she stopped talking, Ruby glanced back at her parents. Her mum had one hand on her heart - the other clutched her father's arm. Both of them looked like they were about to burst with pride.

'Kendra!' said Oli.

Ruby jumped, and then realised several hands had shot up for the next question – and the moment passed.

'Yeah... your male main character is hot!' said Kendra, grinning at her and causing a titter to run around the room. 'I want to know - did you have a mood board of cute guys or something?'

Ruby laughed and felt her nerves disappear completely.

'What can I say?' she grinned. 'Sometimes the research can be *really* tough! But yes - I do make a mood board and-'

'Coming through! Coming through!'

A familiar voice interrupted her mid-sentence. Ruby frowned as she peered towards the packed doorway. People were trying to squeeze themselves out of the way of two newcomers who were edging through the crowd, clearly intent on reaching her.

'What on earth?' muttered Oli, coming to stand next to Ruby.

'It's Bobbie and Ben!' she muttered, watching the two flamboyant publicists elbow their way towards her. 'Save me!' she added with a jokey laugh.

'Helloooo Crumbleton!' cheered Bobbie, as she

came to a halt right between Ruby and Oli, nudging her way into the gap.

The crowd blinked back, clearly not quite knowing what to make of this tiny woman with the huge voice. It didn't help that she was wearing a ridiculous purple bowler hat and a catsuit that looked like it belonged at the Met Gala rather than in a small town bookshop.

'Sorry to gate-crash, but we come bearing news!' said Ben, coming to stand on Ruby's other side.

'News?' said Ruby, her voice low - just for them rather than the crowd.

'Amazing news!' crowed Bobbie. There was clearly no way the terrible two were going to let her find out what was going on in private.

'We are very proud of our Ruby,' said Ben.

'And even prouder to announce…' continued Bobbie.

'Every Little Dream…' said Ben.

'Is going to HOLLYWOOD!' they cheered together.

'What?' gasped Ruby, as the crowd went wild.

'Movie deal, darling!' said Bobbie, reaching up and pinching her cheek.

'You've hit the big time!' said Ben.

'Yeah… so you'd better get things wrapped up here tout suite, my good man,' said Bobbie, patting Oli on the shoulder, 'because we're here to take our girl back to town this afternoon.'

'But… why the rush?' said Ruby. 'I've got questions to answer… books to sign.' Plus she was looking forward to spending more time with Oli - with Caroline - with her parents.

She glanced at Oli, only to find him frowning at her. She wanted to apologise, but there was no chance of that with Bobbie and Ben commandeering the airwaves.

'Well, you'd better make it snappy,' said Bobbie with a shrug. 'You need to get home and get packed. We're off to America tomorrow, darling. Meetings, contracts-'

'Contracts?' echoed Ruby, feeling like her world was starting to spin.

'Yeah,' said Ben. 'They want you working on the script! You'll probably have to relocate for a while - but just imagine - America baby!'

CHAPTER 21

OLI

Oli glanced at his watch. Ten to four. Ruby was gone.

The afternoon train would be whisking her back to London, and then - by this time tomorrow - she'd be on the way to America.

He was happy for her. At least... he *would* be if he thought for one second she was excited about the trip. Talent like hers deserved every opportunity. Movie deals, press conferences, red carpets... the works! But Ruby had just looked haunted. He knew what it felt like to have other people tell you what you wanted – when the reality might be something completely different.

Oli couldn't help but feel like he was looking into a mirror of his past... and he wasn't sure he could deal with losing her again. This time, it would be *her* flying away from him rather than the other way around - but the cracks appearing in his heart certainly felt the same.

Clearing his throat, Oli did his best to ignore the heat building behind his eyes as he focused on the task at hand. Holding the bubble wrap tightly around the precious book, he grabbed a piece of tape to secure it. Then he reached for the roll of brown paper. Two minutes later, he had a neat parcel sitting on the table in front of him, complete with Ruby's address in London. He was about to click the top back on the Sharpie when he paused.

Nope. He wasn't doing this again. He wasn't going to let the distance between them get so big that it would take six years to build a bridge across it. In one deft movement, he added two words across the corner of the package before standing abruptly. He glanced at his watch again. He needed to hurry.

Dashing over to the door, he quickly turned the sign over to "closed" and then turned back to his desk. He'd need to call Brian, and then…

The tinkling of the bell above the door stopped him in his tracks.

'Sorry - I'm closed. Personal emergency!' he muttered, turning with a frown.

'Is that so?'

CHAPTER 22

RUBY

Ruby stared at Oli, her chest heaving as she tried to catch her breath from her mad dash up the hill.

The unknown taxi driver she'd commandeered to whisk her back to Crumbleton had refused point-blank to drive up the cobbles. So, with her head down, Ruby had just made the fastest trip of her life up the hill - and now she was paying for it.

Still, being out of breath wasn't doing anything to stop the fact that she wanted to pounce on Oli like an over-excited puppy.

'You're... you're here?' said Oli, staring at her in confusion.

'I am,' she puffed, grinning at him.

'How... I mean, what... I mean... did you miss your train?'

Ruby shook her head. He really was adorable when he was confused like this!

'The train's gone… and Bobbi and Ben are on it,' she said. 'They're more than a little bit miffed with me.'

'Why?' said Oli, clearly struggling to catch up.

'Because I've just deprived them both of a paid trip to the States,' she laughed. 'I told them I wanted to do the initial meetings with the studio online!'

'Oh,' he said. 'Why?'

'Because I realised something when I got to the train station,' she said.

'What's that?' said Oli.

'I can't walk away from you,' said Ruby, stepping forward and taking his hands gently - even though she wanted to wrap herself around him and beg him never to let her go. 'I never want there to be all that space between us again. I want to be near you… or… with you.'

'Oh,' said Oli. 'I see.'

Ruby swallowed. It wasn't exactly the enthusiastic response she'd been hoping for.

'Of course, if you don't want…' she said, letting go of his hands just as quickly as she'd taken them. Thank goodness she *hadn't* jumped on him! 'Sorry, I shouldn't have just assumed… and you're on your way out… maybe we can talk later or-'

'I needed to post this,' said Oli abruptly, grabbing the package from his desk and thrusting it at her.

Ruby blinked in surprise before taking the carefully

wrapped parcel. She frowned down at her own name and address scrawled on the front

'Oh,' she said.

'Yeah.'

'A personal emergency trip to the post office?' she shook her head in confusion.

Oli mirrored her movement, shaking his head as a smile spread over his face. 'No - look.'

He pointed at the corner of the package where two words were printed in his looped scrawl.

By Hand

'You were going to-?'

'Follow you,' said Oli simply. 'Because I can't handle all that space between us either. Not again.'

'You can't?

'Nope.'

Ruby stroked her fingers over the two words that meant more to her than anything else in the world right now… because it meant they were both in the same place - in more ways than one.

'What's in it?' she said.

'Only one way to find out,' said Oli.

Ruby nodded, but rather than tearing into the paper like she normally would, she turned the parcel over and carefully peeled off the tape. She had a feeling she'd be saving those two little words… maybe she could turn them into a bookmark.

'It's like pass-the-parcel,' she chuckled, extracting the bubble-wrap-covered-package from inside the paper.

'Yeah well, the music's stopped with you Rubes,' said Oli.

It took what felt like forever to burrow through the layers of bubble wrap, and all the while she could feel the heat of Oli's gaze on her. At last, a familiar book emerged - rich green cloth binding with golden lettering that shimmered under the bookshop lights.

'For me?' breathed Ruby, running her fingers over the stunning copy of Persuasion in her hands.

'I bought it for you a long time ago,' he said. 'For your twenty-first birthday, actually.'

'But... you had it in the shop?' said Ruby, confused. 'It was in the cabinet – Kendra said it was reserved!'

'Yeah, reserved for you!' said Oli with a soft smile. 'I knew I'd finally get the chance to be able to give it to you, and that was the safest place to keep it... until I managed to scrounge up the courage!'

Ruby glanced at the book again and then back at him.

'Thank you. It's beautiful. You know - I wanted to buy this the moment I spotted it!'

Oli grinned at her. *"There could have been no two hearts so open, no tastes so similar."*

'Impressive memory there!' said Ruby, her voice thick with heat and emotion.

'Yeah well, I had a good tutor,' said Oli. 'Question is, do you remember the rest of the quote?'

'"*No feelings so in unison, no countenances so beloved.*"'

'Show off!' chuckled Oli. 'But it's the next line that's been haunting me for six years.'

Ruby swallowed and then continued. '"*Now they were as strangers; nay, worse than strangers, for they could never become acquainted.*"' She shook her head. 'Yeah well, dear Jane had to get it wrong sometimes, didn't she?'

'Wrong about Anne and her Captain,' said Oli with a nod.

'Wrong about us too,' said Ruby. 'At least… I hope she is.'

'It's like I told you when you found me in here instead of Reuben,' said Oli. 'You know me, Rubes. In fact, you knew the real me even before I did. We're not strangers or worse than strangers.'

'Then… what are we?' said Ruby.

'Us?' said Oli. 'We're… home.'

EPILOGUE

CRUMBLETON TIMES AND ECHO - MAY 24TH

What's On This Week

Darts at the Dolphin & Anchor, Wednesday 7.30pm

Join our thriving team - beginners welcome, and you won't be the only one. We've got everyone from celebrity authors to university lecturers to our very own bookseller learning the game. Any questions, contact Brian Singer

A Very Special Odd Object Win!

Huge congratulations once again to Sally Hutchinson on scooping this year's Odd Object Cup! As previously reported, the stunning win broke Iris Tait's seven-year streak. Sally's incredible Roman dodecahedron, which she dug up in her own back garden, was a truly incredible find. In exciting news - with help from the county's Finds Liaison Officer - the artefact is now on its way to the team at the British Museum.

Classifieds
WANTED: Cosy House For Two Local Bookworms

Long term only.
Preferably inside the City Gates.
Home office and plenty of space for bookshelves are a must.
Contact Oli or Ruby at Crumbleton Bookshop.

THE END

ALSO BY BETH RAIN

Seabury Series:

Welcome to Seabury (Seabury Book 1)

Trouble in Seabury (Seabury Book 2)

Christmas in Seabury (Seabury Book 3)

Sandwiches in Seabury (Seabury Book 4)

Secrets in Seabury (Seabury Book 5)

Surprises in Seabury (Seabury Book 6)

Dreams and Ice Creams in Seabury (Seabury Book 7)

Mistakes and Heartbreaks in Seabury (Seabury Book 8)

Laughter and Happy Ever After in Seabury (Seabury Book 9)

A Quiet Life in Seabury (Seabury Book 10)

In A Spin in Seabury (Seabury Book 11)

Living The Dream in Seabury (Seabury Book 12)

A Big Day in Seabury (Seabury Book 13)

Something Borrowed in Seabury (Seabury Book 14)

A Match Made in Seabury (Seabury Book 15)

Seabury Series Collections:

Kate's Story: Books 1 - 3

Hattie's Story: Books 4 - 6

Standalones: Books 7 - 9

Lizzie's Story: Books 10 - 12

Upper Bamton Series:

Upper Bamton: The Complete Series Collection: Books 1 - 4

Individual titles:

A New Arrival in Upper Bamton (Upper Bamton Book 1)

Rainy Days in Upper Bamton (Upper Bamton Book 2)

Hidden Treasures in Upper Bamton (Upper Bamton Book 3)

Time Flies By in Upper Bamton (Upper Bamton Book 4)

Standalone Books:

How to be Angry at Christmas

Crumbleton Series:

Coming Home to Crumbleton (Crumbleton Book 1)

Flowers Go Flying in Crumbleton (Crumbleton Book 2)

Match Point in Crumbleton (Crumbleton Book 3)

A Very Crumbleton Christmas (Crumbleton Book 4)

Little Bamton Series:

Little Bamton: The Complete Series Collection: Books 1 - 5

Individual titles:

Christmas Lights and Snowball Fights (Little Bamton Book 1)

Spring Flowers and April Showers (Little Bamton Book 2)

Summer Nights and Pillow Fights (Little Bamton Book 3)

Autumn Cuddles and Muddy Puddles (Little Bamton Book 4)

Christmas Flings and Wedding Rings (Little Bamton Book 5)

Crumcarey Island Series:

Crumcarey Island Series Collection: Books 1 - 5

Individual titles:

Christmas on Crumcarey (Crumcarey Island Book 1)

All Change on Crumcarey (Crumcarey Island Book 2)

Making Waves on Crumcarey (Crumcarey Island Book 3)

Fool's Gold on Crumcarey (Crumcarey Island Book 4)

A Fresh Start on Crumcarey (Crumcarey Island Book 5)

WRITING AS BEA FOX:

What's a Girl To Do? The Complete Series

Individual titles:

The Holiday: What's a Girl To Do? (Book 1)

The Wedding: What's a Girl To Do? (Book 2)

The Lookalike: What's a Girl To Do? (Book 3)

The Reunion: What's a Girl To Do? (Book 4)

At Christmas: What's a Girl To Do? (Book 5)

ABOUT THE AUTHOR

Beth Rain has always wanted to be a writer and has been penning adventures for characters ever since she learned to stare into the middle-distance and daydream.

She recently moved to a windswept, Scottish island, and it is a dream come true to spend her days hanging out with Bob – her trusty laptop – scoffing crisps and chocolate while dreaming up swoony love stories for all her imaginary friends.

Beth's writing will always deliver on the happy-ever-afters, so if you need cosy… you're in safe hands!

Visit www.bethrain.com for all the bookish goodness and keep up with all Beth's news by joining her monthly newsletter!

facebook.com/BethRainBooks
twitter.com/bethrainauthor
instagram.com/bethrainauthor

Printed in Great Britain
by Amazon